**Terence Toh** writes articles by day and fiction by night. He has written arts and culture articles for various publications, including a major Malaysian English daily, for many years. He was the editor of Fixi Novo's *PJ Confidential*, and his short stories have appeared in many local and regional anthologies, including *KL Noir: White*, *Lost in Putrajaya*, *Cyberpunk Malaysia*, *Hungry In Ipoh* and *KL Noir: Magic*. He has also written two Boh Cameronian Arts Award-winning stage musicals.

# FIXI NOVO MANIFESTO

1. We believe that omputih/gwailoh-speak is a Malaysian language.

2. We use American spelling. This is because we are more influenced by Hollywood than the House of Windsor.

3. We publish stories about the urban reality of Malaysia. If you want to share your grandmother's World War 2 stories, send 'em elsewhere and you might even win the Booker Prize.

4. We specialize in pulp fiction, because crime, horror, sci-fi and so on turn us on.

5. We will not use italics for non-American/non-English terms. This is because those words are not foreign to a Malaysian audience. So we will not have "They had *nasi lemak* and went back to *kongkek*" but rather "They had nasi lemak and went back to kongkek". Nasi lemak and kongkek are some of the pleasures of Malaysian life that should be celebrated without apology; italics are a form of apology.

6. We publish novels and short-story anthologies. We don't publish poetry; we like making money.

7. The existing Malaysian books that come closest to what we wanna do: *Devil's Place* by Brian Gomez; and the Inspector Mislan crime novels by Rozlan Mohd Noor. Look for them!

8. We publish books with the same print run and the same price as those of our parent company, Buku Fixi. So a book of about 300 pages will sell at RM20. This is because we wanna reach out to the young, the sengkek and the kiam siap.

CALL FOR ENTRIES.

Interested? For novels, send your synopsis and first 2 chapters. For anthologies, send a short story of between 2,000-5,000 words on the theme "KL Noir." Send to info@fixi.com.my anytime.

# Toyols 'R' Us

Winner of the 1st Fixi Novo Malaysian Novel Contest

Terence Toh

*Published by*
**Fixi Novo** *which is an imprint of:*
**Buku Fixi Sdn Bhd** (1174441-X)
B-8-2A Opal Damansara, Jalan PJU 3/27
47810 Petaling Jaya, Malaysia
info@fixi.com.my
http://fixi.com.my



**Toyols 'R' Us**


First Print: May 2021

Cover and layout: Teck Hee
Consultant: Alyssa Mohamad & Ted Mahsun

ISBN 978-967-2328-55-1
Catalogue-in-Publication Data available from the National Library of Malaysia.

*Printed by:*
Vinlin Press Sdn Bhd
2 Jalan Meranti Permai 1, Meranti Permai Industrial Park
Batu 15, Jalan Puchong, 47100 Puchong, Malaysia

*For Shin Dhee*

*Not a toyol, but you stole my heart*

# 1

## March 25, 10pm.
## Bukit Sinar, Kuala Lumpur.

If there was anything Inspector Khairul hated, it was when people died at home.

It was an irrational feeling, and he knew it. In some ways, after all, that was the most fitting place to die. But that was the exact reason Khairul hated it. Home was supposed to be a place of refuge, protecting you from the wrongs of the world. You were supposed to be safe there. If Khairul had his way, death would never be allowed to touch you at home.

And that went double for murder.

Khairul hated doing house visits. He had an uncanny knack for sensing which houses would reveal a nasty little dead surprise within. Like a spider sense, if you will. But one of those nasty-ass spiders that feasted on corpses.

And right now, his spider sense was going crazy.

Beside him, investigating officer Corporal Jairuz was fiddling with a pair of bolt cutters. A rusty lock at the gate was the only thing keeping them from entering the house.

There was a smile on Jairuz's face. How was he so calm, so carefree? The man had barely half his experience in the force. Yet here he was, casually breaking into a house as if it were second nature. Celaka, he was even whistling a jaunty tune! The Siti Nurhaliza classic "Percayalah", although he was slightly off-key.

*Ha! Off-key!* Khairul laughed to himself. How appropriate for someone trying to break a lock.

An hour ago, the station had received a distress call. A guy named Haris bin Harun had not turned up at his office for the past two weeks, no notice given. All phone calls to him had gone unanswered.

This was his last known residence. That was why they were here now, at this unassuming little terrace house in Bukit Sinar, with a search warrant. Khairul had requested to come along. This case, he had a hunch, could be connected to a string of cases he had been investigating recently.

And judging from how the other cases had turned out, he sincerely hoped he was wrong.

*The employer had called in the missing person*, Khairul reflected. Was he truly concerned about his employee's welfare? Or the fact that he'd have more work without this one employee? Years of dealing with the dark side of human nature made Khairul doubt even the purest of actions.

There was a loud crash. Jairuz had cut through the lock; it fell to the floor. He pushed open the gates gingerly.

"Dipersilakan, Tuan." Jairuz bowed in mock reverence, a stupid grin on his face. He was a tall, slightly chubby man, with prominent sideburns right out of the seventies. His wavy hair visibly glistened with gel.

"Eh, ladies first," Khairul said.

There were old newspapers lying on the porch, some decayed by rain. Haris was probably an older gentleman. Not many young people subscribed to newspapers nowadays. There was a row of potted plants by a nearby wall; many were dead or withered.

Jairuz had already entered the house; his muddy boots left prints on the floor. Khairul almost felt bad, before realizing that the houseowner would not have to worry about cleaning up.

For there was a nasty smell in the air, one he recognized from the countless house calls he had done. It was faint, but it was there: a hideous staleness reminiscent of meat gone bad.

The smell of a corpse.

The smell grew even stronger as the two policemen walked into the house. Khairul regretted having had a late lunch before coming.

The house was small, and very tidy. Very little dust on a couch and coffee table, which took up most of the hall. Framed paintings of landscapes on the walls. A few Malay novels next to a lamp on a small bookshelf. Khairul immediately started taking photographs. Jairuz, on the other hand, went further into the house.

It was barely five minutes before Khairul heard the corporal scream.

"Boss! You need to see this!"

Khairul ran to his partner, who was in one of the bedrooms. He stifled a gasp as he opened the door.

A body was lying on one of the beds. Male, probably in his fifties with short, curly hair. He wore a black shirt and tattered jeans.

What was most striking about the corpse, however, was its expression. His jaw was slack open, and his eyes bulged. They looked like they would pop out of their sockets at any second. It was beyond a doubt that this was the source of the smell. It emanated off the body in waves, so powerful it made the two detectives feel like passing out.

It was almost as if he had been terrified to death.

"No cuts or bruises anywhere else on the body." Jairuz did a quick check, trying not to retch. "No visible bullet or stab wounds. Apa berlaku ni?"

Just then, he gave a cry of shock.

"What is it?" Khairul demanded.

Jairuz, trembling, pointed at the corpse's bare left foot.

There was only a stump of flesh where his big toe would have been. Someone— or something— had hacked it off. It was still bleeding.

"Not again," Khairul sighed.

# 2

## March 27, 1.30pm.
## La Risoto Boulangerie, Bangsar.

"Mail!" Harun rose as Ismail walked nervously into the restaurant. "Wah wah, so long time no see!"

"Assalamulaikum, Harun," Ismail gave him a hug. "You're looking very good!"

"Eh, don't have lah." But the large smile on Harun's face showed he was more affected by the compliment than he let on.

It wasn't empty flattery, anyway. This really was the best Ismail had ever seen his cousin. Usually, Harun barely cared about his appearance, walking around with unkempt hair and a scraggly beard. His usual outfit was torn jeans and a ragged old T-shirt of Black Sabbath or some other old band. And it wasn't like he even listened to them: Harun had been a hardcore nasyid fan ever since they were kids.

Today, he could barely recognize his cousin. Harun's hair was neatly combed, and slicked with oil. He was clean-shaven, and wore a jacket over his dark blue shirt and jeans. He was carrying one of those handbags for men that seemed to be super fashionable nowadays. Gold rings, one with a gem almost as large as a durian seed, adorned his right hand. This, combined with his large frame, made him look like a Petaling Street rip-off of a Marvel movie villain.

Had he struck the lottery? Or been promoted to some high-flying new job? Knowing how much of a slacker his cousin was, Ismail couldn't see the latter happening.

"How about you? Enjoying life?" Harun said, and Ismail laughed as he rubbed his expanding belly. He had put on a bit of weight since last Raya.

"OK lah. Putri, you know how well she cooks," Ismail replied as he and Harun took their seats.

Ismail was tall and portly. He sported a thick mustache, which he had been keeping since secondary school. His wife constantly nagged him to shave it, saying it made his face look as if it were perpetually under attack by a very hairy caterpillar. But he refused to listen to her. This mustache made him look *distinguished.*

He had worn his best shirt for this occasion. A red long-sleeved Armani which had been going for 30% off at a clearance sale two years ago. It no longer fit him as well (it bulged a little in the stomach and he could no longer do the top button without choking himself) but Ismail still wore it. The damn thing had cost a bomb.

La Risoto was packed: it was, after all, smack into lunch hour. The tables of the popular Bangsar eatery were occupied mostly by men in business suits or blonde expatriates in brightly-colored T-shirts and shorts. Waiters in white jackets walked briskly through the area, carrying plates of delectable-looking food. Music floated through the air: some sappy classical piano tune.

"I have to say," Ismail said as he and Harun put on their napkins, "I was very surprised when you messaged me. Kenapa lah, suddenly invite me for lunch?"

It could hardly be said they were close. Indeed, they only saw each other twice a year, Hari Raya and their grandmother's birthday.

"Well, I thought it would be good to catch up a bit. I hardly ever see you. Plus, I have something amazing I want to share," Harun said. He picked up his menu. "I hope you like Italian food. This is my favorite restaurant. Come here before?"

Ismail shook his head.

There was a reason he had never entered La Risoto. The place was halal, and many review sites had gushed about how delicious the food was. But the portions were small, and their prices would set you back an arm, a leg, and possibly a kidney or three. One plate of pasta and drinks could easily eat up one-tenth of Ismail's meager salary.

"Oh, it's a pity. The lasagna here is to die for!" Harun laughed. "What will you be having?"

Ismail's eyes automatically headed for the cheapest thing on the menu.

"A Caesar salad, please," he said, pronouncing it 'Kay-ser'. Harun winced at the mispronunciation.

"You can't be serious!!" his cousin exclaimed, so loudly that customers at the next table turned to look at them. "You're a man! Not a rabbit!"

Harun smiled. "Don't worry, cousin. Today's meal I belanja."

And then, ignoring Ismail's protests, Harun ordered three plates of pasta, two main courses, a soup and two desserts. Thinking of the exorbitant price almost made Ismail lose his appetite.

"Eh, we don't have to order so much you know," Ismail's voice dropped to a whisper. "We can finish ke?"

"Don't worry," Harun smiled. "Can bungkus!"

"There's enough to bungkus for a whole kampung!" Ismail shook his head. "How can you afford all this? I thought you're still not working?"

"I'm not," Harun said.

"Then how did you get all this money? Which bank did you rob?" Ismail braced himself for the worst.

"Eh, don't be silly lah," Harun laughed. "Why go to all that trouble? Dangerous, tau tak?"

He grinned. "Okay, cousin. What would you say if I told you there's a way to make huge amounts of money? Without going to work?"

Ismail groaned. "Ya Allah. I should have known this was coming!"

"Eh, where are you going?" Harun gasped as Ismail stood up. "I haven't told you anything yet!"

"This is where you try to recruit me right?" Ismail said, untying his napkin. "My God, I'm so stupid! Which one is it? Clamway? Multigem?"

Harun tried to interject, but there was no stopping Ismail's tirade.

"I've heard them all before. I kena so many times already! I look gullible, is it? Or poor? Should have known lah, suddenly call me out of the blue! Meet-up konon! Stupid MLM. I never thought my own cousin would do this to me! Well, you can take your MLM and—"

Everyone else in the restaurant was staring. A distracted waiter at the next table overpoured a glass of sparkling water, so taken by this spectacle.

"Don't be stupid!" Harun was red in the face. "This has nothing to do with MLM, okay?! I hate those guys too!"

"Then what is this about?" Ismail demanded.

A waiter came over to check if everything was okay, and Harun quickly waved him away. He turned back to his cousin, and lowered his voice. "I have another way to earn money. One which requires almost no effort. Just pay a small price and the returns are huge."

"I'm not interested," Ismail said.

Harun shook his head. "Aduhai, Mail. You're among family lah. You can be honest, no need for ego." He edged closer to Ismail. "I've spoken to Mak. She told me you're a clerk at this office on Jalan Chan Sow Lin. And I know how much clerks make."

"It's okay," Ismail protested. "I make enough."

"Yes," Harun smiled. "I'm sure you do. But is enough really enough for you?"

Just then, as if on cue, another waiter arrived, with two plates of pasta.

"Okay, let's talk about this later," Harun said. "Let's eat first."

Reluctantly, Ismail agreed. He was starving, and the food was smelling exceedingly good.

"Mmm." Harun licked his lips after biting into the lasagna. "This is damn good, right?"

Ismail nodded. He couldn't talk, all he wanted to do was savor the delectable dishes in front of him. It was no wonder the food was this price; it was some of the best he had ever tasted. The bolognese sauce alone—oh, the rich aroma, the generous helpings of meat mixed with the ripe tomato flavor! He wondered how Italians didn't go around in a constant state of food orgasm, if all their cuisine was like this.

"Just enough cannot ever get you this, right?" Harun said, and against his will, Ismail found himself nodding. "You work so hard. You deserve a lot better. What car do you drive?"

"Hey," Ismail said, in between mouthfuls. "No need lah, mention all that."

"Secondhand car, right? I'm sure the repairs every month are very expensive," Harun said. "Don't you want so much better? A bigger house? Nice vacations?"

Ismail was silent.

Truth be told, he hated going on social media nowadays. His friends would be posting photos of their new cars, or dinners at fancy restaurants in Sri Hartamas or Kenny Hills with names he couldn't pronounce. They'd upload entire albums of vacation photos on Facebook or Instagram, showing Japan or New Zealand or Iceland or whatever flavor-of-the-month country was popular. Usually with some sickening caption and a dozen idiotic hashtags at the bottom.

Ismail would seethe with envy and resentment as he went through them. He knew he shouldn't even look at them, but somehow, he always did. Like a moth to a flame. He would 'Like' one or two photos in a futile attempt to show he was not affected. And seethe the whole time. Luckily, Facebook did not have a 'Fuck you' reaction or he would have abused it like hell.

Where had their last vacation been? Ismail and Putri had gone to Cameron Highlands. They had a coupon on a two-star hotel, which had shoddy Wi-Fi and a swimming pool overgrown with algae. Non-stop bee farms and cactus patches, and the two had eaten strawberries until they were red in the face. Ismail had no idea who the Cameron of Cameron Highlands was. But if he somehow met him, he would punch him in the face for creating such an awful place.

"And what about Putri? Is she satisfied with what you can give her?" Harun continued.

"Don't bring her into this," Ismail scowled, but he couldn't help but feel a tinge of resentment at his wife's name.

Every month, her excessive spending made them come dangerously close to busting the budget. He could live frugally. Ismail was content with his daily food from the mamak, his T-shirts from the pasar malam. It was Putri and her expensive taste, her expensive shopping trips, her weekly cinema visits and high-teas. Ismail would eat Gardenia bread, and she would eat a Wonderslice honey oregano loaf fortified with calcium and cinnamon crusts. He would drink Milo and she would buy coffee from fancy cafés. And not just normal coffee, mind you. ARTISAN coffee. Whatever the hell that was.

All he wanted was a simple life. Why did he have a wife that made it so difficult?

"Okay, enough with the sales pitch," Ismail said. "What do you want to show me?"

"The answer to all your money woes." Harun grinned.

With that, he picked up his bag from the floor beside him, unzipped it, and passed it to Ismail.

Ismail had no idea what he had expected to see when he peered into the bag. Whatever it was, it certainly wasn't THIS.

There was a yellow container inside, the same size and rough shape as a 1.5 liter bottle. Its top and base were made of plastic, while its middle was transparent glass. There were buttons on its side.

Ismail saw through the glass that the container was filled with murky liquid. And within that liquid was a creature.

It was fetus-like in appearance. The creature's tiny, bean-shaped body was only seven or eight inches high. Large ears, like bat wings, stuck out from the sides of its overly large, almost swollen-looking head. The creature was hairless, and wore no clothing, except for what appeared to be a cotton diaper. Its skin was mottled gray. Tiny hands and feet poked out comically from its body, which was covered with warts.

But what disturbed Ismail most were its eyes, which were huge and crimson, and appeared to gleam—whether this was out of happiness, rage, or something else, he could not guess. It had no nose, but a pair of long slits in the center of its face, atop a small mouth. If Baby Yoda from that *Star Wars* TV show had a child with Voldemort from *Harry Potter*, and that child had then been in a terrible car accident, it would have looked something like this.

Ismail stared at it, his mouth agape. To his horror, the creature was moving; its small mouth opened in what was unmistakably a grin, revealing rows and rows of tiny fangs. It took every part of Ismail's soul not to scream as the creature moved its tiny hands.

Celaka, it was WAVING at him!

"That's Budin." Harun quickly took the bag back, and zipped it up. "He looks happy to meet you!"

"What..." Ismail was still at a loss for words. "What the hell was that?"

"You don't recognize that?" Harun was dismayed. "Mail, don't you remember Nenek's stories? That's a toyol!"

"A toyol? But there's no such thing," Ismail said, before realizing how foolish he sounded. There clearly was one in the damn bag.

"They do exist, Mail," Harun said. "And best of all, one of them can be yours."

"What the hell would I want with one of those?" Ismail exclaimed.

"Aiyo, you memang bodoh lah." Harun rolled his eyes. "You sudah lupa ke? Toyols are excellent thieves. They are great at finding jewels and other types of wealth for their owner."

At this, everything suddenly clicked.

"You mean… this is how you've been getting your wealth?" Ismail's head spun. He wondered if someone had spiked the pasta. What he was hearing made no sense at all.

"Yes," Harun nodded. "These things are GILA! They can smell wealth or money, and can enter any house through a tiny crack. They can even go through keyholes or under the doors of a safe! Every night, I send Budin out, and he always comes back with cool things! One time, he even found a gold necklace with the crest of—"

"That's illegal!" Ismail protested. "Stealing is wrong!"

"Aiyo," Harun said. "You want to give me a moral lesson? Think about this lah. You know why nice guys finish last? Because if you want to be successful, you have to break a few rules."

He took another bite of his pasta, before continuing. "Look. Everyone breaks the rules to get ahead. Morality is for saints or the filthy rich. Either you exploit people, or people will exploit you."

"Amboi, when did you become Oprah?" Ismail said, but Harun kept on speaking.

"Look at all these rich people. Remember your old boss? When you were working at that surveying firm?"

Ismail nodded.

"Do you think he got where he was honestly? Impossible, okay? He definitely had cronies and connections. You read the papers, every day it's some minister or fat cat getting charged for corruption or embezzlement. Our dear former Prime Minister, that one the best example. Stealing billions and billions of our ringgit. And I bet you he's not the only one doing that. He's just the only one who got caught."

Harun sighed. "But let's be honest. If you or I were in their position, we would probably do the same things lah. They have so much power and chances to get rich, why wouldn't you take it?" He took out his bag and put it on the table. "We don't have so many opportunities to get rich like these politicians. So we have to use any advantage we can find."

"No," Ismail said. "It's not right." But his voice was weak.

"With a toyol, you can take money from those who have too much. A lot of rich guys, they're so loaded, they won't even notice some of their stuff missing. Wealth redistribution," Harun replied.

Once again, Ismail's head hurt. He had no idea which was more unlikely: that he was being offered a toyol, or that his normally slacker, conservative cousin was suddenly preaching social justice theories.

"I don't know lah," he said at last. "It sounds very tempting. But also very scary. I mean, it's stealing... what if we get caught?"

"How to get caught?" Harun scoffed. "Toyols are magical. They cannot be caught on video or on CCTV. And you can send them to rob houses up to 20 km away. How is anyone going to track you? And even if, let's say lah, someone catches you..." He wiped his mouth with his napkin. "What are they going to do? Make a police report? Against a toyol?"

Ismail, however, was still doubtful. This frustrated Harun.

"Adoi, cousin," he said. "I'm giving you the best offer ever, okay? Trust me, your life will never be the same again."

Harun raised his hand, and a waiter dutifully appeared. Harun paid for the meal with a credit card— it was so new, it gleamed in the light— before taking his bag and rising.

"OK lah. I have to go for my massage very soon. You think about it, okay? If you want to take my offer, you call this place.

And mention my name. They have this recruitment bonus for loyal customers," Harun said, passing Ismail a business card. "Don't be an idiot, okay? Call! And don't show this card to anyone else!"

And with that, Harun left the table, whistling cheerfully. He twirled a set of keys in his hand—a new car, apparently.

Had that really just happened? Ismail wondered. This was all so weird, so surreal. He examined the business card again. It was so simple, it was almost blank. One side had a phone number. The other, simply this in bold black letters:

**TOYOLS 'R' US.**

# 3

## March 27, 2pm.
## Brickfields Police Headquarters.

"We've got a preliminary report," Corporal Jairuz said. "Same finding as all the other cases."

Khairul frowned. "Just like I suspected."

The inspector was tall and in his early thirties. His hair was cut very short, and his body was toned from regular visits to the gym. This afternoon, he was sitting at his desk, going through case reports while eating a bowl of Family Mart oden.

It was a hot day. The standing fan in Khairul's office was creaking loudly as it whirred. It was on medium—any faster and it would blow around the years and years' worth of documents here. It was an annoyance, but the only relief from the heat: the air-conditioning had been bust for years.

"Cerita semua sama," Jairuz said. "Victim died of almost complete blood loss. Drained like a sponge, barely a drop left. And all from a small wound."

"The detached toe?"

"Where else?" Jairuz said, as he dropped a few sheets of paper before Khairul. "This gives me the creeps lah, Sir. Do you think someone is collecting them or something?"

"Like trophies? Maybe." Khairul shook his head. "Some of these people are really sick puppies." A thought entered his head, and he smiled. "Eh. Maybe the perp is smuggling them somewhere."

"Really?" Jairuz gasped.

Khairul nodded. "And you know how he's transporting them?"

"How?"

"With a…toe truck!"

Jairuz shook his head. "Unlikely lah, sir. Why would he need such a big vehicle for such tiny body parts?"

Khairul sighed as Jairuz took his leave. The corporal was a good man and a fine policeman, but had the comic sensibilities of a block of tempeh. It would probably be an hour or so before he got the joke.

Oh well. Time to start reading.

He put on his headphones, turned on the 'Don't Fall Asleep' playlist on his phone, and picked up the first report.

Something really didn't add up.

'Exsanguination'. That was the word the report used. Apparently some fancy term for 'complete blood loss'. But what could have caused something like that? And why kill a person in this manner?

It seemed like something out of a vampire movie. But weren't they known for attacking at the neck? Perhaps a very, very short vampire?

Worse thing was, these cases were happening quite regularly.

Khairul sighed. He picked up the most recent victim's case file.

Haris Adam bin Harun, 52. A bachelor. Worked at a burger joint in Brickfields. Lived alone, no immediate family members.

Khairul did a preliminary check through the web for anything suspicious. Little came up; the only relevant search results revealed Haris won a fishing competition at Lake Gardens two years ago.

Another run though the usual databases revealed the man had no known ties to any criminal organizations. He was so clean, he could open a laundromat. So why had he been murdered?

A check of his financial statements, however, revealed something interesting. Haris had purchased tickets to London a month ago. On British Airways. Business Class.

This was remarkable. How could a burger seller fly in such style? Even Economy tickets cost a bomb. Did he have rich relatives? Maybe some sort of sugar mummy or daddy? It wouldn't be completely out of the ordinary.

Just then, Jairuz walked back into the room. He placed some files on Khairul's table. "Here you go, Tuan. All the other case files."

Khairul's brow furrowed as he re-read them.

Jessica Chan Leow Fang, 24, student. Discovered dead in her house in Kampung Attap, Kuala Lumpur, a month ago. Cause of death: complete exsanguination, through a detached toe.

Naufal bin Nuran, 43, businessman. Discovered dead in his house in Taman Bukit Desa, Kuala Lumpur, three weeks ago. Cause of death: complete exsanguination, through a detached toe.

Benjy Kuppusamy, 40, unemployed. Discovered dead in his apartment in Kampung Kerayung, Kuala Lumpur, five weeks ago. Cause of death: complete exsanguination, through a detached finger.

At first glance, there was nothing these victims had in common, except the strange way they died. All the cases did not appear sexual in nature, and none involved any element of robbery. Jessica Chan, in particular, was found dead in her locked bedroom, which contained a rich supply of jewelry worthy of an ex-Prime Minister's wife. Absolutely nothing had been taken.

Again, this struck Khairul as strange. *What was a young student doing with such a huge collection of jewelry?*

Whatever it was, Inspector Khairul knew he had better get to the bottom of things. His superintendent was dead set on solving this case soon. He had even removed Khairul from all other pending investigations until this was taken care of.

A serial killer was definitely public interest, which would really put the force in a bad light if allowed to drag on too long. Thankfully, there hadn't been too much attention by the press yet. Victims with missing toes were considered too tame for many of these trashy tabloids.

Just then, his door opened, and Jairuz stepped back in, a sheaf of papers in his arms. He was laughing. 'Toe truck! Gila! Good one, sir!"

"Truly, nothing gets past you, corporal," Khairul said.

"Thank you, sir," Jairuz said. "Any luck with the case?"

"Nothing major. But there's definitely some link between all these victims. Probably financial."

"Well, all the best," Jairuz said. "Here's some additional reports. I'm going out now. There's some clown I need to arrest."

"Adoi, no need to insult people like that lah," Khairul said.

"Eh? Oh, no lah. I mean an actual clown!" Jairuz laughed. "There've been a few reports recently. Apparently, there's this guy dressed as a clown— ya, serius ni— with makeup, big red nose, all. He's going around at night, playing circus music and being creepy."

"Damn. What is wrong with some people?"

"Some people just nothing better to do lah. But it should be a very simple case. How hard can it be to find a clown?" Jairuz stood up and headed for the door.

"Hope so." Khairul shuddered involuntarily. He hated clowns. Thank God he had not been assigned to this case.

"Maybe I'll start looking in all the longkang. There's where they live, right? I remember I saw that movie some time ago-"

Khairul laughed. "Please lah. This is Malaysia. Our drains are so dirty, Pennywise also will choke and die."

# 4

## March 28, 5pm.
## Bellfield University, Subang.

Jing really should have been paying more attention to her Chemistry lecture.

In front of the class, Mr. Wong was droning away about inorganic bonds. This was the subject of Jing's upcoming Writing Credit, and a highly popular topic in the final exams. Ignoring it would be academic suicide.

But it was difficult to stay focused. Her mind kept going back to the previous night. The image of her boyfriend's face, flushed and furious, kept drifting to the forefront of her memory.

"Are you fucking sure?" She had winced at the fury in his voice. *"I want a DNA test!"*

"It's yours, I swear!" Jing had to fight the surge of tears that threatened to burst forth any minute now. "You're the only guy I've ever been with!"

"How do I know?" he had screamed. "How the HELL do I know?"

Tommy raised his hand; for a moment, it looked like things were about to get ugly. Mercifully, he had restrained himself. He was a gentleman at heart, that was why Jing had fallen for him in the first place.

They sat in silence for what seemed like an eternity. Him staring into space, her teary eyes focused on her bedroom floor. Anywhere but at each other.

Finally, Tommy spoke again. "How long have you been pregnant?"

"Four months," Jing said.

"Ah," he sighed. "Well, we have to get rid of it."

"What? You mean… you mean like an abortion?"

"What else?"

"I don't know, sayang. I don't think I'm comfortable with the idea. My pastor always told me—"

"Screw your pastor lah," he said.

He put his muscular arm around her. Jing rested her head on his shoulder, doing her best not to soak his shirt with her tears.

"Look. I really can't deal with a baby now. I've got a bright future ahead of me. I've got my degree, and then my Masters. Plus I plan to try out for the national team next year. I can't risk all that, just because you got yourself pregnant!" Tommy kissed her. "I'll find the best clinic for you, okay? And don't worry, I'll find one that's cheap, because I know you're broke this month." He put his arm around her. "I'm sorry, I know it sounds harsh. But it's better for both of us."

Hot tears dripped from Jing's eyes, soaking the pages of her textbook. She was a short, petite girl, with a heart-shaped face and a mole on her left cheek. Her golden-brown hair was tied in a long ponytail.

*On paper, it all seemed so simple*, she thought. *Just go for an abortion. Delete the little monster growing inside me that would ruin my life forever.*

Yet the thought gave her pause.

Unlike her parents, who sometimes spent more time at church than home, Jing did not consider herself religious. She scoffed (silently, of course) at their constant quoting of Bible verses, their praise and worship songs, their outdated views about issues such as homosexuality. The only reason she went to church was to see her friends, and secretly ogle the more attractively-carved Jesus statues.

Yet it seemed some of her parents' preaching had rubbed off on her. They'd always told her abortion was a terrible sin, depriving the world of an innocent soul who hadn't even had the chance to live. Her pastor always told her that life began at conception. Admittedly he was not the best authority on biology, but what if he was right? What if she was murdering a person that she herself brought into the world?

Before she could stop herself, Jing let out a loud sob. Some of her classmates looked at her in alarm, before turning back to the class whiteboard. They had no time for this: there was an exam soon, for God's sake. Mr. Wong continued to drone on and on, unaware of the turmoil brewing in his student's heart.

It was a relief when class ended. Jing waited until most of her classmates had piled out. She did not want them to see her red eyes and smudged mascara. She was so wrapped up in her thoughts, she did not notice a classmate coming up.

It was Munira Kassim. She was tall and tanned, with wavy brown hair clipped short, and a nose stud. She wore a green button-down shirt and jeans, and her arms were adorned with bracelets that looked like they'd been strung together from thorns.

"Hey, Jing." Munira's tone was kind. "How have you been?"

"Huh? Oh, I'm okay. It's been a rough day."

The two had several classes together, but this was the first time they had actually spoken. Jing and Munira usually hung in different circles. Jing's friends were slightly more 'academic', if it could be called that, a group whose main preoccupations were study groups and scholarships. Munira and her friends, on the other hand, were what Jing's parents often called 'bad company'.

"Well, if you don't mind me saying, you look like shit," Munira said. "Where's your gorilla of a boyfriend?"

"Bukit Jalil. He has training."

Tommy Chan was a state hockey player. There was a major tournament coming soon, and he had been training almost every day over the past month.

"Ah. Well, I think you could use someone to talk to." Munira smiled. "Come, let me buy you dinner. You like Mexican?"

Jing paused for a moment, before getting up. Yes, Munira was peculiar company, but she was right. She needed to talk to somebody, right now.

X

There were few patrons in Sombrero's Mexican Diner, and for good reason. The food was awful—Jing had drunk glasses of water with more flavor than these poor excuses for tacos and enchiladas. And the restaurant's tacky interior didn't help. Desert-brown walls, with poorly-painted murals. Stereotypical caricatures of marimba bands and bandits. It was hard to tell which was more tasteless: its food, or the décor. Yet Jing shoveled her food in her mouth without comment.

Munira, on the other hand, didn't eat much. She spent more time on her cigarette than her food, willfully ignoring the **No Smoking, Señor** signs on the wall.

"So, babe," she said. "What's the story, morning glory?"

And despite her better judgement, Jing opened up to her. There was a relief, after all, that came from unloading your secrets to a stranger. She told Munira about everything that had happened, baby and all.

"Shit, that is awful." Munira shook her head.

"Yeah," Jing sighed. It felt good to have someone agreeing with her. "I really don't know what to do."

"Keep the baby. You sound like you want to. I'm sure you'll be an awesome mother."

"It's not that I don't want to. But I don't know if I can support him! Or her! Kids are bloody expensive."

"Whatever you choose, it should be up to you. You're the one that's pregnant, right? Not Tommy. Your body, your choice," Munira said.

Jing tried not to cry. "I don't know. I just feel terrible, that an innocent child will have to suffer for it."

"It's not yet a child. It hasn't even been born yet," Munira said, in the kindest tone she could muster. She paused. "So, when are you going to see the doctor?"

"Soon, I guess. I need to go check some things out first," Jing replied.

"May I make a recommendation? Go and see Dr. Indira at Hospital Puncak Alam. She's totally professional. And completely P & C. My cousin got herself in a similar jam last year, and Dr. Indira, she really helped her out."

"Thanks," Jing said. "Wow, Puncak Alam is pretty far, though."

Munira smiled. "Just a short LRT ride away lah. Or get your boyfriend to drive you?"

"He can't come, he's got hockey practice," Jing said.

"All the time?"

"Big tournament coming up."

Munira rolled her eyes. "Fiddling around with his stick and balls, the only thing he's good at. Why am I not surprised." She grasped Jing's hand, and squeezed it tightly. "Hey, you know what? Why don't I come with you instead? I don't think you should go through this alone."

Jing beamed. "Thanks. That would be lovely."

# 5

MAR 29, 11AM.
KUALA LUMPUR.

"This should be the place," Ismail said.

"You're kidding me." Putri shook her head. "Are you sure?"

They were standing in front of what appeared to be an abandoned building, smack in the middle of Jalan Tun H.S Lee. Around them, cars whizzed down the road, honking loudly; street vendors peddled kuih and drinks on the street.

The building had a huge signboard on its facade: **BAYIKU INFANT PRODUCTS**. The amount of dust covering it could kill a whole ward of asthmatics. Its walls were covered with graffiti and money-lender ads, and its brown paint was cracked and peeling. Several windows were boarded up, and the ones that weren't were cracked.

"This cannot be right," Putri cursed. "Let me see the address again. You probably mixed up a number or something, knowing you."

*The nerve of that woman! Second-guessing me at every opportunity!* Ismail did his best to stay patient. "Ni memang the right place, sayang. I'm sure. Check the door?"

"You check it out lah!" Putri griped. "So clever, Mr. Navigator!"

Putri was in full makeup with gold earrings, in a black baju kurung Ismail had bought her for their last anniversary. Why she had dressed up, he had no idea. All he had told her was this involved toyols, and would get them rich. He himself was just in a T-shirt and some old slacks.

His wife was a small woman, barely reaching up to Ismail's chest. But what Putri lacked in height, she more than made up for in voice. Her speaking voice was the envy of theater actors everywhere: rich, silvery and loud. Easy to hear even over the bustle and noise of the big city.

This big voice was a wonderful quality for an orator, but a horrible quality for a wife. It meant Putri could call him from other rooms in the house and Ismail couldn't pretend he couldn't hear her. And right now, she was pacing up and down the street, complaining at a deafening volume that people in Alor Setar could probably hear.

"I should have known this was too good to be true! Toyol, konon! What the hell was I thinking?" Putri said. "Let's go home lah. You really kena scam."

Ismail grit his teeth. He took hold of the protesting Putri's hand, and walked her over to the doorway. "Let's give this a try, okay? I'm sure we are in the right place."

Ismail wondered if he was mad. Taking leave, on a busy week day, to follow some mad idea from his mad cousin. How had it come to this? He should have known something was up, by the nature of the call.

Immediately after the dinner with Harun, Ismail had dialed the number on the card. Part of it had been on a whim. Another part had been out of genuine interest. What if this really was legit? If it helped his finances, what did he have to lose?

"Toyols 'R' Us!" a man had answered. His voice was smooth, with a slight English accent. "Now, everybody can own a toyol! How can I help you?"

Ismail had been taken aback—he hadn't really expected anyone to answer. The man on the line, however, seemed to have anticipated this.

"My name is Lewis. I assume that one of our clients introduced you to us?"

"Yes," Ismail said gratefully. "His name is Harun."

"Harun Bakthiar? Oh yes, good man!" Lewis said. "A new customer, but a very good one. He was just here yesterday! I am willing to bet, sir, that you are just as handsome as him?"

"I uh… I think so?"

"Brilliant! Now what's your name? And where are you based?"

"Ismail Baharuddin, Kampung Attap."

"Excellent! You can come visit our main headquarters in KL!" Lewis chirped. "At Toyols 'R' Us, we have packages for people from all walks of life. Why don't you drop by for a free consultation? We can identify which package would be best for you."

"Package?" Ismail was confused.

"What kind of toyol you'd like! We have all types, and can tailor-make the best option for you. Let me just ask you one basic question. What are you hoping your toyol can give you? Is it a life of financial stability? Lavish wealth? Or maybe to pay off a debt?"

"Financial stability, I guess," Harun said. "I'm not greedy."

Lewis laughed. "Sir, there is no such thing as greed. There is only the desire to do better, to earn more! Shall I make an appointment for you… tomorrow morning? Will 11.30am be a good time?"

Ismail almost replied he would be working… however, he paused. He had been slaving like a dog for the last few months. Three other staff had been laid off, due to the company's cost-cutting, and taking over their workloads hadn't been easy. He could sorely use a break, and getting a fake MC would be rather easy.

"Yes," he answered. "That will be great."

"Excellent," Lewis replied. "Now, here is our address. Please take it down."

"Could you just WhatsApp it to me?"

"Sorry. I'm afraid we can't. We don't like to leave a paper trail, you see. The thing about this business is, due to its nature, it has to be conducted in a very confidential manner. So please don't give this address to anyone else," Lewis said. "Also, take down these instructions. You will need them to find us once you arrive at our premises. They may seem unusual, but as we said, confidentiality."

Ismail took down the details.

"Fantastic," Lewis said. "Now then. Anything else you'd like to ask?"

"Yes," Ismail said. "Is what you're doing legal?"

There was loud laughter. "Oh, Encik Ismail, you are very funny," Lewis said. "I'll see you tomorrow!"

And at that, the line went dead.

Ismail and Putri had to step over bricks and debris to enter the building, through a pair of massive iron doors that had long rusted. Vandals and graffiti artists had drawn all over them.

As Lewis had told Ismail over the phone, they were unlocked, and surprisingly easy to push open. It was as if someone had been oiling them regularly.

Ismail and Putri made sure no one was looking, before stepping through the doors. They gasped as they found themselves in a small empty room with a stone floor. It was lit by flickering fluorescent bulbs on the ceiling.

"There! A door!" Putri pointed excitedly.

"Aiyo, never seen a door before is it?" Ismail grumbled as they made their way to another door in the corner. It was barred by a combination lock. "Okay, what's the number?"

"8-6-9-6-5," Putri read her husband's handwritten instructions. The lock opened with a snap. "Wah, sayang, this is so exciting! Like treasure hunt!"

This door, on the other hand, led to what looked like a doctor's waiting room. Sterile-looking couches next to magazine racks and a water cooler. Posters on the walls, announcing things like **The Best Formula for Your Baby** and **Get Vaccinated Now!** The only other door in the room was locked.

"Okay. Now what?" Putri asked.

"Go to the poster next to the water cooler," Ismail read his instructions. "And lift it up. Carefully."

"Yeah," Putri said as she did. She gasped to discover that the poster covered a large, glass-paned window in the wall. It was boarded up from the other side.

"Look at the bottom. Is there a button? Press it," Ismail said.

There was indeed: a large red button, which looked like something out of a cartoon.

Putri pressed it, and there was a loud buzz. Almost immediately, the boards came down, the window opened, and a smiling face appeared on the other side.

"Hello there!" It was a bald man with a white mustache and square-rimmed glasses. He spoke in a heavy Chinese accent. "Welcome, welcome! You found us, very good! Are you here for an appointment?"

"Yes, we are," both Putri and Ismail said.

The old man slapped his forehead. "Stupid question! Why else you want come here, right?" He held out a small plastic container. "Just pass me your ICs, ya? So sorry for all the trouble to find us. But then, fun also right?"

Ismail and Putri did so, and the man took down their details before passing their ICs back.

"Okay, Encik Ismail. Thanks so much. My name is Ah Chuan, so nice to meet you. Now, just go through the door there, ya? It won't be locked anymore. Mr. Lewis will tell you everything. And if you're worried ah, no need! This is the best decision you will ever make."

Ismail was starting to feel like he was in a low budget rip-off of *The Da Vinci Code*. Secret codes, secret entrances, secret organizations! Was all this some elaborate prank?

Ah Chuan was a skinny old man in a frayed, holey black T-shirt and khaki pants. He was missing his right foot, there was a metal prosthetic attached to his knee. Despite this, or perhaps because of this, Ah Chuan moved extremely lightly, hopping and skipping from time to time.

He led them down a long corridor, which led to another door. This led to a lift. Ah Chuan flashed his access card at a wall scanner, and pressed the button to the third floor.

"Okay, Encik Ismail, Puan Putri," Ah Chuan said, once they arrived. "Got to go now. I have a lot of cleaning to do. You just walk until you reach the waiting room, okay? You stay there. Mr. Lewis see you shortly."

He bowed, and gestured for them to leave the lift. Ismail was almost sorry they were parting; his friendliness had been welcome in this strange place.

"Comel lah that guy," Putri said. "I wish my office receptionist was like that."

After a short walk, the two found themselves at another waiting room. A desk, piled with various files and books, and two large couches next to a magazine rack. File cabinets in the corner next to an empty row of shelves. The only thing unusual was that the windows behind the desk were boarded up with planks. Easy-listening piano music was playing from a speaker in the ceiling.

There was a large sign on the wall. A cartoon drawing of a smiling baby with fangs, dressed in a blue loincloth. **Toyols 'R' Us** was written in big, colorful block letters next to it.

"Now what do we do?" Putri said.

"We wait, I guess?" Ismail shrugged.

They took a seat on one of the couches. Putri took out her smartphone, while Ismail turned to the magazine rack. Mostly old *Reader's Digests*, a *National Geographic*, and some women's magazines. One magazine, however, he did not recognize: *BUSINESS BOMOH MONTHLY.*

Ismail flipped through it, only to discover he did not understand any of its contents. 'ENCHANTMENTS FOR

ESPIONAGE: ETHICAL OR NOT?' one section read. 'VIRGIN SACRIFICES: HOW MUCH DO THEY REALLY AFFECT THE STOCK MARKET?' another said. 'EYE OF NEWT SHORTAGE TO AFFECT TRADE WITH CHINA', said another.

The only part he did understand was a section that referred to this very business.

'THE COMMERCIALIZATION OF TOYOLS', the article read. "GROSS PERVERSION OR GROSS PROFITS? YOU DECIDE!"

*"Once, they were looked upon with fear. Toyols, long considered the bottom tier of the Malaysian undead. Gross, misshapen beings, used only by street rats and common pickpockets. Most bomohs would rather be caught dead (or undead!) than be seen with one of these. Two years ago, the Night Police even famously issued statements condemning these beasts. Which says a lot, considering their infamously liberal policies.*

*But that was the past, which as they say, is a different country. Today, toyols are TO DIE FOR: must-be-seen-with fashion accessories on par with Louis Vuitton bags or Enchantro spellphones. Toyol mills like Toyols 'R' Us and Shockabye Baby Sdn Bhd are thriving. Designer toyols can cost a fetus's weight in gold five hundred times over. And it's all thanks to one man..."*

Reading these strange terms made his head hurt. Ismail was halfway through the article, when he suddenly heard something unusual. The piano music had stopped, and another song was playing. Even Putri noticed. She had put her phone away and was now listening attentively.

The singer was a woman. And the song went:

*'Toyols 'R' Us!*
*Baby we're the best!*
*You can't beat us*
*So don't delete us*
*We've got the need-sus*
*Of your fetus*
*We're not kidding around!'*

It was ridiculously catchy; Ismail knew he would be humming it against his will over the next week.

As the song finished, the door opened, and a man stepped into the room. He was very skinny, with a shaven head and sideburns. He wore a blue shirt and red tie, as well as white slacks. What appeared to be an inch-long dagger was hanging from his right ear. He walked over to Ismail and Putri, and shook their hands.

"Hello, hello, Encik Ismail. Puan Putri!" Lewis said cheerfully. He smelled strongly of oranges. "So nice to meet you. My name is Lewis Virgil Gnanasegaran. We spoke over the phone?"

"Yes, nice to meet you too," Ismail said, and his wife smiled.

"We hear that you are interested in buying a toyol," Lewis said. "That's fantastic! And I must compliment you, madam, on your fine figure. I wouldn't have guessed you were pregnant at all!"

Putri's jaw dropped, and Ismail commented hurriedly: "She's not pregnant!"

Lewis groaned. "Oh my god, kepala bapak aku! There I go, putting my big fat foot in my mouth!" He turned to Putri. "I am so, so sorry. Most of the time, whenever a couple comes here, the wife is expecting. I really shouldn't be so presumptuous, I'm so sorry."

"It's okay," Putri said.

"Once again, I apologize, Puan," Lewis said, and bowed his head as if in contrition. In less than five seconds, however, his head had snapped up again, and he was smiling.

"Now then. Thank you for choosing Toyols 'R' Us. It is the wisest thing you can do for your financial future," Lewis said.

He sat on the couch opposite them and took some pamphlets from the rack nearby.

"First things first. Let me just give you a little run-down of our company," Lewis said, pointing to a chart. "I don't know if you've heard, but Toyols 'R' Us is one of the most reputable toyol merchants in the country. The toyol trade, as you might know, has rich historical precedent—it goes all the way back to the Sultanate of Johor in the sixteenth century. There are records of toyol trading with the Dutch East India Company. And today, our company is carrying on this fine tradition!"

Lewis paused as if he expected laughter, however none came from Ismail or Putri.

"We have branches in three states. Each branch conducts its business underground. And as professionally as you could hope for. So don't worry, sir, madam, you're in the right hands."

He bowed his head again. "Also, we're sorry about all this trouble finding us. All these are part of regulations. But it also helps us. Toyols, you see, have a bit of a bad reputation. Many people only associate us with stealing, which is not the case! So whenever anything goes missing in the area, we are the first ones to be blamed. People come after us with torches and pitchforks!"

"I see," Ismail said. "So, uh, can we get a toyol?"

"Whoa, jumping right in, are we?" Lewis laughed. "I like you, sir. Straight to the point."

"First, you have to fill in these documents." He headed to the desk, and pulled out some crisp new forms from its drawers. "These are all about preferences and so on. Helps us get the right product for you. So, if you don't mind, can I ask you some questions?"

Ismail and Putri nodded.

"Excellent. First off..." Lewis now sounded a little more serious. "You both know what a toyol is, right?"

"Isn't that the ghost that flies around and eats people? Around the banana trees?" Putri asked.

Lewis shook his head. "No, madam, that is the pontianak. And we do not deal with those here. Although come to think of it, you may have given me my next business idea!"

"I know what a toyol is," Ismail said. He had heard stories about these little creatures since he was a child. His late grandmother always blamed one whenever one of her kerongsang or a bit of her money ended up missing (although, Ismail had to admit, it was usually him or Harun that was responsible).

"Well, even if you don't, there's a detailed explanation on the form there, please read it," Lewis said. "I warn you, some of the photos are quite gross."

He gave them some time to browse through the material he had handed them, before speaking again.

"Now I have to check: Are you aware that the toyol is the reanimated form of a dead fetus?"

"Yes," the couple said.

"You are aware that it takes black magic to bring one to life?"

"Yes."

"And you are aware that using one is technically against most religions, especially Islam and Christianity?"

There was a pause for a while, before the couple said: "Yes." Ismail was a bit more hesitant than Putri.

"And by the way," Lewis went on. "I am legally bound to remind you there are legal penalties if you use the toyol for criminal means. Illegal use of a toyol can be prosecuted with bla bla bla bla, it's all in the forms. Knowing all this, you still want to go ahead?"

Again, the couple was silent for a while.

Finally, Putri spoke up. "Will it get us more money?"

"Yes."

"Confirm?" she asked.

"Yes, that we can guarantee."

"Then sign me up!" Putri said. She nudged Ismail hard in the ribs, and he too said, "Yes."

Lewis grinned. "Excellent! I like you both. A couple after my own heart!"

After Ismail and Putri filled up their forms, Lewis took them back to the lift and brought them to another floor. There, they walked down a corridor, which led to them another door.

Ismail wondered just how many doors and rooms this place had, and how anyone remembered how they were all linked. You needed a bloody GPS to get around!

This door led to a brightly lit room. There was a large sign on one of the walls: **Toyols 'R' Us Display Showroom**. Next to these words was another cartoon image of the monster baby from the waiting room.

A girl in her early twenties was seated at a counter. Behind her were three tall cupboards, each containing three to four rows of yellow plastic canisters. They were exactly the same as the one

Ismail had seen in Harun's bag at the restaurant. If you squinted a little, you could make out vaguely humanoid shapes in each one.

"Hello, Lewis," the girl stood up to greet them, a huge smile on her face. Her hair was tied in an elaborate braid which reached her waist. She wore a blue blouse, and the shortest skirt Ismail would have thought possible. She was very pretty.

Ismail suddenly felt his wife elbow him in the ribs again. *Celaka, was it that obvious I was staring?*

**DAWN,** her nametag read. **CUSTOMER SATISFACTION OFFICER.**

*She can satisfy me any day of the week,* Ismail thought.

"Hello, Dawn," Lewis said, and he introduced everyone. "Dawn is in charge of getting our customers exactly the right kind of toyol they need."

"Hi, everyone!" Dawn said, smiling widely. "If you need an undead baby, then I'm your lady!" She giggled.

Lewis winked at Ismail. "Also, if you pay extra, you and her can make a fetus of your own. If you know what I mean."

"What?" Ismail and Putri were both shocked, but Dawn was now hitting Lewis playfully. "Please lah, Lewis, don't talk nonsense!" she giggled. But the smile on her face was a lot smaller.

"We're here to get Encik Ismail a toyol," Lewis said. "What do you suggest? An Anggerik? Or maybe one from our Tulip line?"

He passed her the forms the couple had filled in earlier, and Dawn went through them. Her brow crinkled as she read, it was adorable.

"How about an Ixora?" Dawn said. "It's not too fancy, but it's very versatile."

"What's the difference between all of them?" Putri asked.

"Well, different toyols are bred for different uses. The Anggerik, for example, is our basic toyol. He's an efficient thief, but he's not... how do you say this... the brightest? So he can sometimes get lost after you send him out. I mean, he will definitely return, but it may be the following day," Dawn said.

"And our Teratai breed... well, he's not the best at stealing, but he's amazing at causing mischief. Some of our customers want that, you know? Just to cause trouble with their neighbors. They'll hide their keys, turn on lights in the middle of the night, pinch them in their sleep."

"Yerrr." Putri shook her head. "I tak mau!"

"Well, whatever you want, we will have the toyol for you," Lewis said. "We have a top-notch research team. Award-winning, actually. We've combined both elements of magic and genetic manipulation to make quality toyols for every situation."

"For example, our Kemboja breed, they've been trained to plant hidden recorders or cameras. In great demand by politicians," Dawn said. "They were *massively* popular during the last general election."

"But you... I think you want either our Cempaka or Jasmin varieties. The Cempaka is especially speedy. And can carry slightly more than all our other toyols. Our Jasmin, on the other hand, is especially good at finding rings and jewelry. He—"

"I want that!" Putri interrupted. "The Jasmin!" Her eyes were flashing; Ismail could almost see dollar signs in them.

"Ah, yes. That's always a popular choice for ladies," Lewis beamed.

"A good choice!" Dawn said. "I'll get you one!"

She picked out a canister from one of the lower shelves, and brought it to the counter. As it was closer, Ismail noticed its top was sealed with plastic and wood. **TOYOL: KELAS JASMIN**, a label proclaimed in big block letters, next to a serial number.

"Now, you just take this to the counter outside, and after you pay, you'll have your very own toyol!" Lewis beamed. "And soon, you'll be rich!"

Ismail instinctively reached out to take the canister from Dawn, but Putri stopped him. Now it was her turn to be hesitant.

"I'm just curious," she said. "When I buy a toyol… what exactly am I getting?" She nudged Ismail, and hissed: "Mana boleh simply beli-beli? Must check first! How we know they not trying to scam us?"

She probably meant for it to be a whisper. Putri's voice, however, was booming; Ismail realized Lewis and Dawn probably heard every word she said. If they had taken any offence, however, they did not show it: the duo kept smiling.

"Actually, that's a good question, madam," Lewis said. "I really like you. Smart consumer. Dawn, do we have any samples we can show her?"

"We sure do," Dawn said. "Come. Let me introduce you to my best friend." She reached under her table, and pulled out another canister very similar to the ones on display.

"This is Jungkook. He's an Orkid-class toyol. They were used a lot during the war, and are still very popular now. Great for combat or dangerous situations, to disarm people of their weapons. He's also been trained to protect his owner from all kinds of danger. Though, thankfully, he doesn't do that very much now." Dawn pressed a button at the side of the canister, which slightly raised its cover.

There was a slight hiss… almost like opening a carbonated drink. Small wisps of smoke began to flow out from the top. The canister's watery contents started to shake, and the creature within started to rise.

Putri screamed. It was a tiny creature, resembling an ape, but hairless. Tiny claws sprouted from its long arms. Red pupils grew from slits on its face, atop a tiny mouth filled with fangs. Its only clothing was a grubby-looking cloth diaper around its waist. Despite its monstrous face, however, there was something rather… distinctive about this toyol's appearance.

"Wow," Ismail said. "It looks like—" But Putri shot him a dirty look and he shut his mouth quickly.

The toyol leapt over to Dawn, moving with amazing agility, raising two feet in the air with each leap. Dawn picked it up, and it started to lick her face affectionately.

"Here at Toyols 'R' Us, we create the best quality toyols, from the best quality fetuses. We don't just pick off any dead baby from the street… each of our fetuses has to go through rigorous quality control before we even consider it," Lewis said.

"You're damn right!" Dawn said with a smile, and there was something about the way she said this that gave Ismail chills.

Jungkook smiled—it was the ugliest smile anyone had ever seen. It began to trill: *krr-ka, krr-ka.*

"Most toyols from Toyols 'R' Us are extremely intelligent," Lewis said. "Unless you buy the discount models lah. But our research team has trained our toyols to be aware of seventeen types of threats, ranging from policemen to burglar alarms. It knows how to stay out of sight, and in situations of danger, can even vanish."

As if on cue, the toyol suddenly disappeared. There was no flash of light, no puff of smoke—one minute it was there, one minute it wasn't.

Just then, Ismail heard a *krr-ka, krr-ka* from behind him. He whirled around to see the toyol, now leaning against the door.

"Good boy!" Dawn said, and the toyol bounded joyfully toward its mistress. She held out a finger, and the toyol bit into it. It lapped up the small drops of blood that formed.

"Yerrrrr." Putri made a face. "I have to feed it blood?" She nudged her husband again. "That one your job."

"Can it speak?" Ismail asked. He wanted to sit down; this was proving a bit much for him.

"They can say simple things. Maybe a word or two. Think of him as a very ugly parrot," Lewis laughed. "But don't worry. He can understand you perfectly. Our research team has arranged it so he can understand commands in English, Malay and Mandarin. We're still working on Kadazan, Cantonese and Tamil. We're very 1Malaysia!"

Jungkook walked up to Ismail and Putri, and extended its clawed hand. It smiled as Ismail, after the greatest of hesitation, shook it. Putri was still too terrified to touch it.

"So how do you use this thing?" Ismail asked.

"Well, it's very easy. You take one home. For your first use, you open the canister and recite this doa we give you. This is to let it know you are its master," Lewis said. "Then, after that, it's up to you. You can use it every night… it sleeps in the day. Just open the cover, and the toyol will come out. You can order it to steal for you. It will never disobey."

Lewis cleared his throat.

"You bought the Jasmin model. Those are quite fast and strong. As I mentioned, they have a nose for jewelry, so they will bring back a lot of rings and bracelets. And don't worry… it knows the difference between pasar malam ones and the real kind. He can also bring back money... the Jasmin variety has been trained to identify seven major currencies, including the US dollar and the Japanese yen!"

"Wah, memang canggih." Ismail was impressed.

"How exactly does it find the stuff to steal?" Putri was still a little skeptical.

Lewis laughed. "You'd make a great journalist, madam. Always asking the tough questions!"

He cleared his throat. "How toyols find wealth is one of the greatest supernatural mysteries out there. Even with all our expertise and study, we don't exactly know how they do it."

Dawn piped up. "All we know is toyols have a very powerful sense of smell which can pick up gold, jewels, money, and other items of value. We think it's because of its nature as a stillborn baby. Since it was created through an act of love, it is drawn to things that humans love."

"Indeed, there are studies showing that fetuses created through love produce bigger and stronger toyols than those conceived through force," Lewis continued. "You can talk to our toyol specialists if you want, they can tell you a lot more."

"Toyol specialists?" Ismail asked.

"Oh yes. Each of our toyols will be marked by special anti-sorcery runes, cast personally by our specialists. This is to prevent them from being affected by other spells. No magic will affect them, other than your initial summoning spell," Lewis said.

When he was done, Dawn whistled. Jungkook waved them goodbye with a smile, and ran back to his canister, his arms dragging on the ground as if he was a gorilla. He jumped inside it with a tiny splash, and Dawn closed the cover again.

"I think this is great," Putri said. "Just one thing though. Does the toyol need to be… so ugly?"

"Sayang." Ismail frowned, but Lewis was laughing.

"An excellent question! You'll be surprised at how often that comes up. People nowadays… they don't just want a toyol, they want to brag about it in high society! So don't worry! We can arrange a good-looking one for you!" he exclaimed.

"You can check out our luxury Sri Cendana collection. Fetuses made from the best-looking genetic material possible. We have Siamese, Caucasian, and even Pan-Asian donors! Remember when Pan-Asians used to be all the rage? We even managed to grab a deal with a Hong Kong supermodel. We can make toyols even more good-looking than you are! Interested?"

"Actually, it's okay," Ismail said. He forced a smile at his wife, who scowled at him. "I think a regular toyol will do?"

"Brilliant," Lewis smiled. "So the Jasmin model, then?"

Ismail turned to his wife, but her mind was already made up. "Yes, yes, we'll take it!" she said.

"Excellent," Lewis said. "Now, this is under the Friends loyalty scheme, so if you know anyone else who is interested, tell them to mention your name whenever they come here. You will get 25% off future purchases. I think Harun will definitely be coming in to upgrade his Anggerik soon."

Dawn passed him a calculator. Lewis started keying figures in.

"Also, it comes with a one-year guarantee. So with registration fee, and SST… it should come to this amount."

He showed them the calculator, and Ismail gasped. It was more than he and his wife made in six months.

"Wow," he gasped. "That's very expensive."

"Well, the process of creating a toyol is not easy, you know. Needs a lot of science and magic. You think just like making nasi lemak?" Lewis laughed. "Besides, a toyol will gain money back for you! It will pay for itself really fast!"

"Do you accept installments?" Ismail asked half-heartedly, knowing even if they did, they would not be able to afford it.

"Well, you can pay us a deposit first, and then pay the rest over the next year. But if you agree to this, make sure you do pay," Lewis said. "If not... well, we have ways of ensuring we get our money."

"If you can't afford them, then maybe a cheaper model?" Dawn suggested. "The Anggerik?"

"Tak mau." Putri shook her head. She pouted, making her look like a five-year-old child. "I don't want something so ugly."

"We will think about this and get back to you," Ismail said, and his wife gave a small cry of despair.

"You're walking away from the best decision in your life." Lewis shook his head.

"Isn't there another way?" Ismail asked desperately. "Some other payment method?"

Lewis paused for a while. He held his chin, looking as if he was thinking deeply. And then he spoke.

"There is maybe one thing you can do. Most of our costs come from the creation of a fetus, which if taken from our stock, must affirm to our standards. So that costs a lot. But if you supply your own fetus... we can close one eye a bit. All we would need to do is the procedure, and that will be much cheaper. So if you find one, come back lah. If not, maybe raise some more money...Anyway, I have a meeting soon, so goodbye and please take care."

With that, he waved to Ismail and Putri, and walked out of the room.

# 6

## March 29, 2pm.
## KL Sentral LRT Station.

"It's hopeless," Jing sighed. "I really don't see any point."

"We mustn't lose hope," Munira said.

The girls had earlier gone to Hospital Puncak Alam. There they had learnt, unfortunately, that Munira's doctor friend was no longer working there. She and her husband moved to the United Kingdom last year.

"That's why lah she never picked up her phone," Munira sighed.

They had taken the train to Nu Sentral for lunch. Jing would happily have had a few drinks to drown her sorrows, if not for Munira reminding her that alcohol was bad for babies.

Now, they were on their way home. It was sweltering. Jing started to regret her choice of clothes: a thick wool sweater and jeans. But it was the baggiest, most shapeless outfit she had. She knew she would have to get used to hiding her pregnancy if this abortion thing didn't work out.

Jing couldn't help but feel extremely judged. She knew it was probably psychological, but it felt that everyone she passed, from the LRT staff to the makcik selling kuih on the street, knew what she had done, knew her for what she was.

*A dirty slut who couldn't keep my legs closed.*

She found herself sweating profusely. Her heartbeat quickened as she and Munira lined up to reload their Touch n' Go cards, queuing up behind a middle-aged Malay man and his cross-looking wife. After that, they headed to the LRT. Jing couldn't wait to get home.

"So. What's next?" Munira said.

"I don't know," Jing said, as the girls boarded the near-empty LRT. They both took a seat, opposite the couple from before and a pink-haired teenager whose loud music was audible even through her headphones.

What a terrible position to be in. Abortion could only be done in very specific cases in Malaysia. Munira and Jing had spent the previous night researching it. While the laws here were a lot less restrictive than in other parts of Asia, it was still not easy to get an abortion. It could only be done in cases where the pregnancy was endangering the mother's life, or her physical or mental well-being.

Jing highly doubted she was in this category. As far as she knew, her pregnancy seemed to be going quite well. A nasty thought entered her head: How easy would it be to accidentally fall down the stairs, or take a little tumble on the road? Surely a little bump might be all that was needed…

Immediately she felt horrible for thinking that, and quickly forced the thought out of her mind. Doing that would really make her a murderer.

Anyone who induced a woman to miscarry could be sentenced to up to three years in jail. Seven years if it was after the fourth month of pregnancy. And this law included the pregnant mother herself. Jing had been reduced to tears, reading about Nirmala Thapa, a Nepalese migrant who was arrested in 2014 for trying to get an abortion while six weeks pregnant. She was eventually acquitted, thankfully. But that was before an initial conviction; she was the first woman in Malaysia to be found guilty of an illegal abortion since 1989. And Jing doubted she could handle the stress and trauma of the full Malaysian court system, stigma and all.

There were safe, reputable abortion providers out there. The only problem was finding them. Here, health professionals had been known to refuse to terminate pregnancies, due to personal values or religious beliefs. Some of them tended to be extremely kaypoh, poking and prying about irrelevant issues such as sexual habits and marital status. This sometimes led to women going from hospital to hospital, trying to find a doctor willing to help.

Apart from that, cost was also a factor. Anywhere from five hundred to four thousand ringgit. And Jing simply did not have that kind of money.

*This is ridiculous,* Munira fumed. Unwanted pregnancies were a thing that would happen no matter what. The least that could be done was to provide safe, accessible health services. But in this country, where even baby-dropping hatches were considered to promote sin, that was apparently too much to ask for.

Jing didn't even realize it, but she had started to cry. The other passengers in the LRT looked at her with a mixture of pity and curiosity as tears ran down her cheeks, ruining her mascara. But their opinions were the last thing Jing cared about right now.

"Hey." Munira put her arm around her. "It's okay. It's okay."

"I've ruined my life." Jing tried her best not to start sobbing. "I'm so stupid. And now everything is fucked."

"No," Munira said, calmly, and embraced her friend. "You haven't ruined your life, okay? If anything, the only person to blame is that stupid boyfriend of yours. He did this to you, and he should be the one taking responsibility. He should be here with you instead of me. We'll get through this. All right? I promise. No matter what happens, everything will work out fine. We'll find another doctor. Even if we have to go to a thousand."

"Maybe I should just have the baby," Jing said. "Put it up for adoption or something."

"It's your choice, Jing. Whatever happens, I'll help you," Munira said.

"Thanks," Jing said gratefully.

Just then, the Malay man from the seat opposite walked up to them, his wife following closely. "Hello, excuse me," his voice was nervous. "Are you okay?" His wife held out a grubby-looking packet of tissues.

"No, I'm not," Jing said. "I'm having a very bad day."

"I didn't mean to overhear," the man said. He lowered his voice. "But… am I right that you are pregnant?"

"Yes," Munira snapped. "She is pregnant! And that is none of your business!"

The man was taken aback for a while, but quickly recovered. "No, no, I'm not here to judge you! Jangan bimbang. Let me introduce myself. My name is Ismail, and this is my wife, Putri."

He held out a business card. "I know this may sound weird, but listen to me. There may be a way we can help each other."

Curious, Munira took the business card, and showed it to Jing. There was a phone number on one side, and a simple phrase on the other.

**TOYOLS 'R' US.**

# 7

## Mar 29, 9pm.
## Taman Sri Gerhana, Kuala Lumpur.

Another late night. Khairul yawned as he drove his police cruiser down a near-deserted street.

Not that he was complaining. He loved late hours.

He turned up the volume of his 'DON'T FALL ASLEEP playlist', and the screeching of Justin Bieber boomed loud in his ears.

Khairul had never been a morning person. He could never wake up before noon without a small army of alarm clocks. And hardly anything exciting happened at 8am anyway. Even criminals liked to sleep in.

No, give him the night, with all its darkness and secrecy. The prospect of constant excitement was one of the main reasons he became a police officer, despite his family suggesting law or engineering. He'd certainly had the brains for those other careers. But not the heart. The thought of sitting at a desk all day depressed him immensely. He'd rather be out on the streets, tracking down criminals, doing his best to ensure that justice was served.

His family had been extremely surprised when he told them his policeman ambitions. Khairul had always been considered the family comedian. (Or the family joke, according to some of his least favorite relatives.) Everyone knew him for his laidback attitude and habit of making terrible puns at the most inappropriate times. To hear he wanted to become a police officer seemed like a bad joke that no one was getting.

But years of watching *Gerak Khas* and *Police Academy* films had planted a seed in the soul of young Khairul Munawir. He longed for their exciting lives, filled with gunfights and car chases. These TV policemen, who risked their lives to uphold law and protect the innocent were the coolest people he had ever seen.

Few people had expected him to really put in an application to PDRM. Fewer still believed he would pass the entrance exams, and eventually rise to the rank of Inspector.

Of course, one of the first things Khairul learned on the job was that real-life police work was absolutely nothing like what was shown on television. But that didn't really matter: Khairul soon found he had a knack for investigating, and impressed everyone with his rapid rise up the ranks.

Well, **almost** everyone.

His father's face suddenly flashed in his mind; Khairul felt a tinge of sadness. The two of them had not spoken for several years now. Ever since Khairul had told him he was going into the police force. The old man had dreamed of his eldest son becoming an engineer. This had resulted in a series of awkward family reunions and silent Hari Rayas, where he refused to even look his son in the eye.

*Maybe I should call my father*, Khairul thought. Stubborn as he was, he missed the old man.

Khairul was starting to wonder if perhaps his father had a point after all. The job, while thrilling, was starting to take its toll. Khairul had been a good police officer, or so he'd like to think. One of the youngest officers to be accepted in the Major Crimes

Division in years. He'd helped crack a few really serious cases. But all these long hours, with relatively low pay, was making the job lose its luster.

Five long years. Exciting years, true, but the robbery and murder investigations were starting to lose their appeal. His previous case had involved a particularly sadistic killer in Gemas who bound and tortured his victims before slashing their throats. The guy was caught, but not before he had killed six people.

Six people; he had failed. This haunted Khairul every night.

Perhaps he needed a change of environment. Try another job, hopefully one that paid a lot better. He heard there was much to be made in private security.

But he would think about all that later. Right now, he had a case.

Half an hour ago, the precinct received a desperate call from nearby Taman Sri Gerhana. A neighbor was reporting screams and strange noises coming from one of the houses. Most people would have dismissed this as someone too immersed in a horror movie, perhaps. But Khairul knew how tidak apa your average Malaysian was. Most of them would rather die than get involved in something that wasn't their business. If someone called to report screams, those screams were probably something to worry about.

Taman Sri Gerhana looked like your average KL neighborhood. Khairul knew very little about it, except that it was a predominantly Chinese, lower-income area. There was also a night market here every Sunday with an excellent laksa stall.

Khairul parked. He recorded the spot on his Routefinder app, in case he ever needed to come back here: TAMAN SRI

GERHANA CRIME SCENE. He knew how bad he was with directions.

The Taman's residents watched suspiciously behind their gates as Khairul walked down the street. Many of them seemed to be watching Chinese dramas. He could hear loud dialogue in Mandarin, accompanied by music, even from outside. The smell of sewage wafted through the air—probably a clogged drain somewhere. At one shabby-looking terrace house, two teenage boys took a photo of him on their smart phone, trying to look subtle but failing.

Khairul paid little heed to any of these, and kept walking.

Suddenly, he stopped. He was overcome with uncertainty; his flesh was cold, and there was an unpleasant stinging on his arms and neck. He was sweating. His head swam, and he nearly fell. Khairul had to lean against a nearby telephone pole to keep his balance.

And out of the corner of his eye, he saw her.

She was a tall, slim woman with long brown hair. There was a large pendant in the shape of a scorpion around her neck. She wore a green blouse, cropped to expose her shoulders, and dark jeans. She stood about five meters away from him, by the gate of one of the houses.

The woman was staring at him intently. Khairul felt uneasy. An image flashed in his mind: that of a cobra spotting a rat within striking distance.

Khairul had to force his gaze away. He closed his eyes, and a dark agony, like a fiery migraine, filled his head. When he could finally open his eyes, she was gone.

He blinked. It was as if someone had turned up the brightness on the world for a few seconds, before quickly turning it back to normal. He was nauseous, but forced himself not to puke. Those damn kids were still recording him, and he did not want *Puking Cop* to be the top viral video on YouTube tomorrow.

The house the caller complained about was easy to find: No. 23, Jalan Cempaka Larut, Taman Sri Gerhana. A small corner house on a side street. Small compound, big enough for one car, next to an unkempt patch of grass and potted plants. Large windows, covered with dust. A mailbox filled with bills and flyers.

Again, his death spider senses tingled.

There was another policeman outside. Young-looking, Malay, with thick glasses. Khairul recalled seeing him off and on at the station. A newer recruit, and the investigating officer for this case, most probably.

The policeman saluted as Khairul presented his identification.

"Good evening, Inspector," the policeman said. "Major Crimes handling this?"

"Yup," Khairul said. "No one inside?"

The officer shook his head. "I've been calling for ages. No one replying."

"All right," Khairul said. "Cordon off the area. I'm going in."

According to the investigating officer, this place belonged to a Jaafar Kanan, a teacher at a nearby secondary school. It seemed an average, if rather messy, home. There was a thick layer of dust on almost every piece of furniture. Food wrappers and half-eaten bowls of cereal in the hall. Baby cockroaches skittered all over the floor, fleeing as Khairul approached.

The first step of every crime scene investigation was securing scene dimensions. Where was the focal point of the crime, and what was a good parameter for evidence?

Khairul immediately started looking for a bedroom. Experience had shown him that most crimes in the home took place there. Criminals used them for everything **other** than sleeping.

The kitchen and master bedroom were very untidy. Nothing of interest in either of them. It was in another smaller bedroom, however, that Khairul found some very interesting things.

A plush-looking sofa and footrest, in front of a single bed and a huge plasma screen TV. This already set off warning bells— how could a secondary school teacher afford such luxury?— but it was something inside one of the nearby wardrobes that really surprised him.

Cash. Hundreds of RM50 and RM100 notes, all held together by rubber bands. Oddly, all the bills looked crumpled and folded; they had definitely been used before. Which was odd. This ruled out forgery, and made it very unlikely to be a bank robbery, where notes would be crisp.

Some notes were badly stained, from what appeared to be curry.

"Well," Khairul said. "Looks like it really is a case of dirty money."

He was sad no one was around to hear this badass pun.

There had to be at least one to two million ringgit here. *Looks like Encik Jaafar wasn't just your average sweet school teacher. Probably something to do with drugs. But what did he have to do with the other cases?*

An evil thought entered his mind. Surely no one would notice if he took home a handful or two of cash? No one would miss it, and his rent was coming up soon.

Khairul shook the thought out of his head, and opened another wardrobe.

There was a yellow canister on one of the shelves. It was filled with a strange, odorless liquid. Khairul took a few photos of it.

Just then, there was a loud clatter. Wary, Khairul drew his pistol. The noise came from the room next to him.

Khairul opened the door and stepped in. He gasped.

Most of the room was shrouded in the darkness of the night. But with the meager light from outside, Khairul could make out a figure on a bed. A middle-aged man with glasses, clad in a singlet and sarong. It was Encik Jaafar. His face in an expression of agony. He was clearly dead.

There was a creature at the foot of the bed, chewing at his toe.

Khairul wanted to scream. The creature turned to look at him; it was barely a few inches tall. It had large glaring green eyes and fangs that glittered from a slit mouth on its huge head. It wore a grubby-looking loincloth, and only seemed to have one hand. Its left arm ended in a stump. Jagged claws, however, protruded from the fingers of its right hand.

"*Chirik!!!*" it hissed at Khairul, and raised its single arm as if it were a boxer. It was almost cute.

Khairul didn't hesitate. He fired a shot, but the creature leaped away so fast, the bullet hit the bedsheets instead. It was almost a blur as it moved.

He raised his gun again, but the creature was on the attack. Now it lunged at Khairul, almost landing on his stomach; fortunately, he managed to shoot it in time, knocking it to the floor. The creature did not bleed, or even look injured. Instead, it rose swiftly and pounced again.

Khairul had no time to shoot again. He could only scream as the monster landed on his left leg, plunging its fangs into him. He yelled; the hideous pain made him want to faint. Weakened, he dropped his gun and collapsed. Summoning all his strength, Khairul grabbed the creature— its skin was cold and slimy— and tried his best to pull it off him. But the creature's fangs were still embedded in him like fishhooks.

Just then, the door opened again.

To Khairul's shock, someone entered. It was the woman he had seen earlier.

Khairul wanted to shout a warning, but the woman suddenly pulled out her phone from her pocket. She shouted a phrase that sounded foreign, and the end of her phone started to glow. The glow focused into a bright blue beam, which shot out at the creature. The creature released its bite, but it was too late: the beam flew right into it and burst into silver sparks, knocking it away.

"Thank you," Khairul could only say as he and the woman rushed to the monster. It was curled up on the floor, its skin blackened, and there was a burning smell in the air. It wasn't moving.

"Is it dead?" Khairul asked as the woman picked out what appeared to be a large flask from her satchel.

"It was dead to start with," the woman said. Her voice was deep but youthful-sounding.

"There was a container like that in the other room," Khairul said. "In the wardrobe."

The woman nodded. "Of course. That's probably where he stored them."

"What exactly are these things?" Khairul asked.

The woman shook her head. "I would have thought even a biasa like you would recognize a toyol. A kwee kia, a misdreka. The soul of an unborn fetus, brought back to life to cause havoc."

She turned to him. "You must have a lot of questions. I'm Detective Fara Astaka. I'm with the Night Police. Bukit Aman Occult Investigation Unit.

Khairul laughed. "What? Bukit Aman doesn't have such a unit!"

"Careful now. Do you want to be arrested for impeding an investigation?" Fara said. Her voice was stern. "Of course we have a unit. You just don't have the clearance to know about it. How do you think we investigate all the occult crimes in this country? Rogue bomohs, pontianak attacks, orang minyak… you think they let just anyone deal with those?"

She pulled out a license from her bag. Khairul had to admit, it did seem pretty legit. Out of courtesy, he handed over his license to her as well.

"Inspector Khairul Munawir," Fara said. The impassive expression on her face did not change. "Nice to meet you. I've been working this rogue toyol case for the past two months. I received a tip-off that there was someone using them here."

"Do a lot of people get murdered by toyols?" Khairul asked.

"No," Fara said. "This is the first time we're seeing this. Usually, they're just used for burglary."

She opened the flask and using a pair of tongs, gently placed the creature inside it, before closing it again.

"What are you doing with that?" Khairul asked.

"Oh don't worry, inspector. I'm not going to run away with it. I need to go and get it dispelled. That's the only way we can both proceed with this investigation." She yawned.

"Okay, it's getting late. I tell you what. I'm off tomorrow, but I'd still like to discuss the case. Why don't you meet me at Arun's Mamak for dinner tomorrow? The one in Bangsar, not Subang. Let's share all we know about the case. I think it will take both of us to crack it."

# 8

## March 29, 11.50pm.
## A house in Taman Asyik, Kuala Lumpur.

The website's headline proudly proclaimed: *Malaysian scientist makes research breakthrough for cancer vaccine!* Below it was the photo of a smiling woman in a lab coat holding up a test tube.

Razif knew immediately what he had to do. Fingers twitching, he quickly left a comment on the page.

*Tudung mana tudung? Betina jalang!*

He smiled to himself as he pressed the 'Enter' button. That should knock her down a peg or two. The nerve of these women. Going around thinking they are so great. Flaunting themselves in sexy clothes. The nerve!

Razif took a sip of Coke. He was short and scrawny, with a shock of messy, uncombed hair. A big-eyed anime girl was tattooed on his left arm.

Another lazy night at home. He leaned back in his computer chair and closed his eyes. He had been at his computer for almost six hours. Games and porn had taken up most of that time.

He checked his phone. No new WhatsApp messages.

Razif sighed. He had such good feelings about that last company. The interview had gone so well. He had been jobless for three months now, and was almost desperate for employment.

*Maybe they'll get back to me tomorrow*, he thought hopefully. To clear his mind, Razif decided to indulge in another favorite online pastime. He logged out of his personal Facebook account and signed in onto another one. On this account, his name was Chan Ah Fook.

'Chan Ah Fook' had only four Facebook friends: Razif had Friend requested over fifty random people, and these were the only few kind (or apathetic) enough to approve him. His few posts were news reports or game requests. And he was a fan of only one page.

Local politician Aini Hazliza. A youth representative of an opposition political party.

There was a new update on her page. A photo of her, smiling, with about a dozen other women around her. 'Launching of the Empowered Woman's Initiative campaign at Nu Sentral. Drop by if you have time!' the caption read.

Razif groaned. These bloody feminist bitches. Going all around with their toxic man-hating and bloody empowerment nonsense! He loathed Aini Hazliza. Loathed her half-moon glasses, her flowing, un-tudunged brown hair, loathed her sharp powersuits and well-manicured hands. Women like her, confident and fearless, made him feel powerless, insecure, insignificant. They gave women false ideas, making them believe they were too good for men like him.

He typed his favorite comment below that photo as well:

*Tudung mana tudung? Betina jalang!*

Frankly, Razif did not care at all about headscarves, or know anything at all about the rules surrounding them. In fact, he actually liked looking at women's hair. What he enjoyed was humbling these proud women. And how could they answer back when he was backed up by rules of religion? He enjoyed the thrill it gave, being able to tell them off. After all, he'd never dare to say this to them in real life.

Razif yawned. It was still too early to sleep. What should he do now?

*Ah, well, perhaps some more porn.*

He had his hand halfway down his boxers when the door suddenly opened.

It was his freaky housemate, Ignatius.

"Dude!" Razif screamed. "Don't you ever knock?"

"Sorry," his housemate said. He was a large, tanned guy with a sharp nose and very bushy eyebrows. His voice had slight traces of an American accent. "Just came to return this."

In his hand was a copy of *Mysteri*, a local bilingual tabloid revolving around the bizarre and the supernatural. **ANJING SAYA KAHWIN JIN AIR!** the cover stated in lurid green block letters.

"Just put it on the bed, man," Razif snapped. "And get the fuck out!"

"I was actually wondering," Ignatius said. "Do you have any more issues? Especially ones with those little creatures."

"What little creatures?"

"The ones made from dead fetuses. That crawl around and steal. The 'yolo' or something."

"Toyol!" Razif rolled his eyes. "I don't know lah. I'm not a librarian! Come back later. If I find any I'll give you."

"Okay." Ignatius turned toward the door. "By the way, how is my order?"

"I told you lah. My cousin is very busy now. Got in trouble with the Thai police."

"Thanks," Ignatius said matter-of-factly. He left, closing the door behind him gently.

*Thank God*, Razif sighed. He just wanted to enjoy one of his favorite videos (*BUSTY STEPSISTER TAKES ON FIVE HORNY MEN AT ONCE!*) in peace.

He made sure his headphones were plugged in. The last time he hadn't, Ignatius had burst into the room, horrified at the sounds. He had given Razif a long, long, LONG lecture about purity and how he should pluck out his eyes for looking at filth and other such nonsense. Razif had to remind him that unlike in the United States, here no one was not allowed to preach Christianity to him. That shut him up, thank goodness.

Razif couldn't stand Ignatius. Such a bizarre dude, always muttering Bible verses and whatnot. He didn't seem to have a job; he would just stay in his room all day, and only emerge to go to God-knows-where at night. Sometimes while wearing weird costumes. The only good thing about him was that he was one of his cousin's top customers.

He was thinking of moving out soon. There was this really nice place in Kelana Jaya he was looking at. Near the LRT station, and best of all, in close proximity to a girls' school. Talk about constant cuci mata!

But honestly, anywhere would be good, if it meant not having to live with Ignatius anymore. That weirdo gave him the creeps.

Razif sighed. The video was just not doing it for him today. There were only so many times you could watch a multiple gang-bang before it got boring.

*Oh well.* He grinned as he opened his wardrobe. There was something inside he had been working on for months.

*Time for some big fun.*

# 9

## March 30, 2pm.
## Toyols 'R' Us, Kuala Lumpur.

"Damn," Munira whistled as they went through the final door. "Someone really went to a lot of trouble to hide themselves!"

"Yeah." Ismail nodded. "Gila lah, all this effort."

"Aiyah, told you already ma," Ah Chuan smiled. "Must keep this place secret!"

Jing was silent as the four of them followed the one-legged man into the Toyols 'R' Us reception. She still wasn't sure she trusted this man Ismail, or his wife, Putri. But right now, they were the best chance she had.

Ah Chuan brought them to meet Lewis, a dapper-looking man in a dark coat, before taking his leave. Lewis told them he would be their 'Toyol Attainment Manager' for the session, whatever that meant. He grinned widely as he shook hands with both Munira and Jing.

"Hello, ladies!" Lewis said happily. He was wearing a very strong orangey perfume—you could smell him from a mile away. "Thank you for coming to Toyols 'R' Us! Let me reassure you that you are definitely making the right choice when it comes to family planning. We care about you, and your fetus! Now, which of you is pregnant?"

Jing raised her hand shyly, and Lewis came to her. Without asking permission, he put his hand on her belly. Munira glared, but the man didn't seem to notice.

"Ah! It feels like it's about four months old?" he asked. "A good age for a toyol," Lewis added after Jing nodded. He then turned to Ismail and Putri, a big smile on his face. "I can't believe how lucky you are, managing to find a fetus at such short notice! Truly it is written in the stars."

Written in the stars, it seemed. What kind of heavenly bodies would be so cruel to triumphantly herald the death of an innocent?

Jing felt faint. She wondered if it was not too late to back out. To just go home and lock herself in her room and not come out until next year. Yes, it would not solve her issues. But then again what would?

She began to wonder if she had been too impulsive in agreeing to this.

The first thing Jing did when she got home after meeting Ismail and Putri was make a call. She lay on her bed, braced herself, and called a familiar number.

"Hey, baby!" was the first thing Tommy said as he picked up. "Have you done the you-know-what yet?"

"No," Jing said. "I've… gotten a very unusual offer."

And slowly, she related everything the couple had told her. There was a long silence after she finished—so long it was terrifying. If not for the sound of his breathing, Jing would have thought they had been disconnected, or worse, he had hung up.

"Sayang," Tommy finally spoke. "How can you believe all that shit?"

"I don't know. It might be worth a try! Who knows—"

"Don't be ridiculous. Toyols, it seems! There are no such things, Jing! That guy is trying to scam you!"

"No!" Jing protested. "I don't think he is! I'm just saying, we should think about it. If it can help us, then why not, right?"

"Can you please stop talking nonsense??" Tommy was choking on his rage. "Look, just go for the abortion! It'll solve all our problems! Why is that so difficult for you?"

His voice turned icy. "If you don't, sayang, I will leave you. I'll buy a ticket and fly back to Sabah. You'll never see me again. You want that?"

"No, baby," Jing was trembling. How could the love of her life be so cold?

"And you remember those photos you sent me that time? The 'special' ones? Before I leave, I'll forward them to everyone I know," he went on. "Especially your parents. And your church. You want that or not? Then go for the *FUCKING ABORTION!* Stop being so selfish and get it over with!"

Jing couldn't believe her ears. "Me, SELFISH?" she screamed into the phone. "EXCUSE ME?? YOU WERE THE ONE WHO DID THIS TO ME!"

Jing hung up. She leaned against her bedroom wall, breathing heavily, before closing her eyes and counting to ten. *No use getting angry. Stay calm.*

Strangely, she was not crying. Jing usually wore her emotions on her sleeve. The smallest things could set her off into tears; she wept at cat food commercials, for God's sake. Yet oddly, there was no sorrow in her heart now.

What there was instead was a red-hot rage. Her breath was heavy as she remembered Tommy's smug, condescending voice, his threats. How DARE he speak to her that way?

Jing screamed. She grabbed a vase on the table, and flung it against the wall; it shattered into a thousand pieces. Her hands twitching in anger, she picked up her phone again.

"Hello? Munira?" she said. "Let's go."

Lewis led them to a lift, and they went up to the sixth floor. After that, he led them into what looked like a hospital waiting room. A woman in a nurse's outfit was waiting for them at a counter.

"Hello, Dawn," Lewis said, as he ushered the four of them into seats nearby. "Are we all good?"

"You're the girl we met yesterday! The Customer Satisfaction one!" Ismail exclaimed. "Wow, you are also a nurse?"

"Dawn does a lot of work here at Toyols 'R' Us," Lewis said.

Munira and Jing gasped. There was a toyol beside her. Ismail and Putri recognized it as her beloved Jungkook. The toyol grinned, and waved at them.

Jing turned white. THIS was what her baby was going to be made into?

"Holy shit," Munira said, and took out her phone.

"Don't bother," Lewis laughed. "Unless they're in their canisters, they can't be caught on camera or video."

"The place would fall apart without me," Dawn said. "I'm covering for my colleague. He's out on a harvest."

Part of Jing wanted to ask what exactly this meant. However, words suddenly failed her. She had the tendency to freeze up among strangers or people in authority. She must have looked very worried, as Munira took her hand and squeezed it.

"Hey," she said. "It's going to be all right."

Lewis asked them to take a seat while they got ready. Ismail and Putri sat opposite them on the couches. They did not speak to each other. Putri leafed through some old magazines from a rack nearby, while Ismail fiddled with his phone.

*Well, I guess making a baby is definitely not an option for them*, Jing thought, and smiled despite herself.

At the counter, Lewis and Dawn were having an argument.

"Have you tried calling him?" Lewis's voice was loud. "This is ridiculous!"

"That was the first thing we tried!" Dawn's eyes were flashing, her cheeks red. "Vellu has not been replying to any of our messages! Qahin even went to his place yesterday. No one was in!"

"Fuck lah, why the hell are we even paying him?" Lewis cursed. He seemed to suddenly catch himself and turned to face his guests, his face apologetic.

"Sorry. Please excuse my French. Things have been tough here as of late. The doctor who was supposed to be doing your procedure is not replying. We're not sure where he went."

"Some people are just lazy," Putri sympathized. "Just like my husband. Never do any work!"

"You know," Jing hazarded a try. "If this is not a good day, maybe we should come back another time."

"No, don't worry," Lewis smiled. "We've got another person who can perform the delivery. He's one of our research scientists."

"Is he competent?" Munira asked.

"Oh yes," Lewis said. "Everyone in our company is the best! Our Dr. Hafiz, he was in the medical line originally. I think he was a gynae for a while! But he joined Research after we had a vacancy there. He hasn't done a delivery in years, but no worries! Once you do it once, you never forget, right?"

Dawn smiled. "I guess this is your lucky day!"

After about fifteen minutes, Dawn told them the surgery was ready.

According to Lewis, you were allowed to accompany Jing into the operating theater. Putri declined the offer, claiming those places made her jittery. Ismail decided to stay with her.

"I'm already on Level 70 of my game lah, I need to beat this boss," Ismail said, holding up his phone.

Munira, of course, said she would go with Jing.

Dawn led them into another room. It contained a few cabinets, each about waist high, next to a chair. The chair reminded Jing of the ones in dental clinics, and she shuddered again. Dentists. Probably the only things more frightening than the procedure she would be going through now.

Dawn handed Jing a drab-colored sarong. "Take off all your clothes, and put this on," she said. "There's a changing room over there."

With that, Dawn took her leave, and Jing went to get changed.

As she unbuttoned her blouse, Jing thought about leaving. The more she reflected, the more senseless her actions seemed. What was she thinking, signing up for this procedure that seemed dodgy as hell?

*I should just walk out of here right now,* Jing thought as she wrapped the sarong tightly around her. *Go for the abortion. Go back to Tommy, and move on with life.*

But the memory of the phone call lingered in her memory, and she frowned.

*What the hell, Jing. What do you have to lose?*

"Everything good?" Munira asked.

"Yeah," Jing said, as she left the changing room, the sarong wrapped around her. The material was soft and pleasant against her skin. "It should be good… okay, no, crap, it's not!"

Munira hurriedly turned away as her friend's sarong fell to the floor.

"How do you people wear these things?" a red-faced Jing asked as Munira helped her secure her sarong.

Just then, the door opened, and a portly man stepped in. He wore black-rimmed glasses and a surgical scrub. A kopiah sat atop his head.

"Hello," he said cheerfully. "My name is Dr. Hafiz. You Miss Tan Jing Lee?"

"Ya, saya," Jing said. She walked over to him, doing her best not to let her sarong fall down. The two shook hands.

"Nice to meet you!" Hafiz said. The door opened again, and Dawn walked in, carrying a glass on a tray.

"Okay," she said to Munira. "You need to leave now. The procedure is going to start."

"Take care," Munira said, and she gave her friend a hug. "Don't worry. I'm sure it will all go well."

With that, she left.

"Okay," Jing said. She motioned to the chair. "Should I lie down?"

"Ah, sila minum dulu," Hafiz smiled.

Jing accepted the cup with gratitude; it was some kind of sirap bandung. It was sickeningly sweet, with an aftertaste reminiscent of peppermint.

"That drink is also to help with the procedure. Don't worry if you feel a bit sleepy, that is perfectly normal," Hafiz said.

Jing shivered. Was all this really legitimate medical procedure? Or had she just walked into a very, very bad situation?

"Come cik. Lets begin," Hafiz said. He moved over to his desk and pulled out a file from a drawer. "Just lie down and relax."

"I heard you haven't done this in a while?"

Hafiz laughed. "Yes, that's true. But don't worry, okay? You are in good hands!"

"What exactly are you going to do?" Jing asked.

"Standard stuff lah. A mixture of science and sorcery. I'm going to remove your fetus, and place it in a mixture of herbs, cow's blood, and tanah kubur. That's earth that we've taken from a graveyard. Add some poniba salwa oil, and leaves from the pokok ara. Then we'll have our minyak toyol. I'll just need to chant the proper incantations, and all will be done," Hafiz said.

"All this is safe?"

"Yes, of course! I went to Universiti Bomoh Kebangsaan! Top of my class!" He smiled. "Now close your eyes. Ini sangat cepat punya!"

The drink was beginning to kick in. Jing suddenly felt her vision growing blurry. Her head suddenly felt heavy.

"Wow…that drink…it's very strong." It was hard to speak, her tongue was tingling madly.

"Relax," Hafiz cooed. "Semua okay."

Her eyelids heavy, Jing lay down on the couch. The world spun all around her. Hafiz gently straightened her body. Even in her half-addled state, Jing could feel him loosening her sarong.

"Don't worry," Hafiz said again. "Ini semua biasa. Nothing to be scared about."

He picked up a long blade with serrated teeth, and began rubbing it with a greenish ointment.

Hafiz walked toward her with the blade. Jing's whole body froze, and she began to tremble.

*Stop!* She wanted to yell. *I've changed my mind! Get that blade away from me!* But the tingling on her tongue had intensified. It was as if a dozen needles were being forced into it at once. She could only close her eyes and try to block out the pain.

Hafiz made a cut on her stomach: mercifully, it did not hurt as much as she expected. But it still stung. Jing wanted to raise her hand, force Dr. Hafiz away. But she was too weak to move. She tried to scream, but she could not open her mouth. All her senses were failing: her sight was fading, while every sound around her seemed hollow and loud.

Suddenly, it was cold... her entire body began to tremble violently. To her horror, there was suddenly a sharp pain in her stomach, and she felt her lower body start to contract, harshly and painfully, completely against her will.

But the worst was yet to come. Dr. Hafiz was now slathering her breasts and stomach with a strong-smelling oil. It smelt foul, like fish left outside too long, and made Jing feel nauseous.

He was not gentle at all, his hands moving in fast and careless strokes. Jing's only relief was that he was not groping her; she would have been powerless to stop him.

It was just then she felt a strange rumbling in her stomach. Like hunger pangs, but far, far worse.

*There's something moving inside me.*

It seemed to be moving upwards, going from her stomach toward her chest, its movements faster and more pronounced with every second. Jing's sight had faded to almost nothing at this point, but her hearing had amplified to supernatural levels. It was almost as if she was travelling through a tunnel: every little sound, from Dr. Hafiz's breath to the touch of metal against her skin was hideously loud, booming and echoing all around her. The pain in her stomach had increased and was unbearable.

It was just then that Hafiz spoke for the first time during the operation. And he said the most terrifying word he could have said in this situation.

"Oops."

*Oops? What do you mean, oops? What the hell is happening?* That was what Jing wanted to scream. But she barely had any energy left.

Tears filled her eyes. She took a deep breath, and surrendered to the darkness. The last thing she remembered was Hafiz bending over her, a scalpel in his hands.

Jing awoke with a gasp. Every part of her throbbed with pain, and there was a hideous ringing in her ears.

It took all she could not to weep. She did not know which was worse: the pain in her temples, or the pain in her stomach. It was as if a horse had kicked her in the gut.

Someone had switched off the lights. Her eyes, still brick-heavy, struggled to adjust to the darkness. She was still naked; her body trembled with both fear and cold.

Jing struggled to get off the chair. As she did so, her foot kicked against a bucket on the floor. She bent over and threw up. No matter how hard she vomited, however, she was unable to get the sickly-sweetness out of her mouth.

There was a surge of pain again. Jing ran her fingers over her stomach to discover a long, jagged scar, about seven inches, running from the bottom of her right breast to her groin. Surrounding it were dozens and dozens of scratch marks, tiny but deep.

For a moment, she feared the worst. *What the HELL have they done to me?*

There was no light in the room whatsoever. And yet, Jing realized she could see through the shadows. Everything was crystal clear. It was as if someone had applied a tinted glass filter on her eyes. Was this some side effect of the operation?

Just then, the door opened, and Dawn walked in. She was carrying the sarong from just now.

"Weargh happtarepo theprosi waszassess!"she said happily.

"What?" Jing was confused.

"Oh, sorry," Dawn spoke slower and louder, enunciating each of her words thoroughly. "We. Are. Happy. To. Report. Procedure. Success."

Jing took the sarong and wrapped it around herself gratefully.

"Your. Hearing. Has. Been. Affected," Dawn said. "Take. Deep. Breath."

Jing did so. Mercifully, the ringing in her ears subsided. At the same time, the world around her became shrouded in shadow; apparently, her enhanced eyesight was also fading.

"Better?" Dawn asked.

"Yeah." It felt so good to hear normally again.

"Do you want to see what we created?"

Jing thought for a while. Somehow, she had a feeling she would not like what she saw. And yet, after all she had just gone through...

"Yes," she finally said.

"Okay. Give us a minute," Dawn said, and stepped out of the room.

In less than a minute, she returned. With her was Munira, who was carrying a candle. Hafiz walked slowly beside her. Behind them were Ismail and Putri. Jing blinked from the sudden illumination.

"Congratulations!" Munira said happily. "We have a toyol!"

"Really?" Jing said, unsure how to feel. "Where is it?"

Hafiz smiled. "Tengok atas."

Jing did, and screamed. Immediately Ismail and Putri followed.

In the dim candlelight, she could make out a creature, holding on like a monkey to a rod that protruded from the ceiling. It was small, slightly bigger than a kitten, with a big, bulbous head, and large hands on long, spindly arms.

Hafiz smiled. "They like the darkness." He whistled, and the creature leapt, with surprising agility, onto the floor.

Up close, Jing noticed there was a small mark in the shape of a star on the toyol's head. It was almost cute. Could she really call it a birthmark if this toyol had technically never been born?

The doctor petted her toyol. "A success! And look at that mark on its head! Unik betul!"

He smiled. "I know a dozen or so people who would love to own this guy. Not just bomohs, okay; a lot of people use them nowadays! In fact, there's one prominent minister who bought three from me! Nak tau siapa?"

Jing did not know how to react. She had known this was coming. Munira had explained to her exactly what to expect. But still, actually looking at it— this freakish creature she once thought to be just from ghost stories, now come to life!— was utterly bizarre.

Stranger still, however, was how she was finding it *cute.*

"Ya Allah, hodohnya." Putri shook her head, and Jing was suddenly overcome by a wave of anger. Who was *she* to be passing judgment on other creatures?

"Let me have him," Jing said. "I want to hold him."

"What?" Hafiz was taken aback. "Are you sure? Isn't it—"

"Give him to me. I am his mother, after all."

"Just whistle."

Jing did, and the toyol scampered toward her on all fours. It was surprisingly light. Jing tried not to laugh as the creature nuzzled against her. Feeling its rough skin against her hand was oddly satisfying.

"Mak!" it cried.

"It can talk!" Ismail exclaimed.

"Yes, they are quite intelligent," Hafiz smiled. "We're not sure how, but a lot of toyols learn human speech without even being taught. They pick it up in the womb or something."

There was a warmth in her heart Jing didn't know how to explain. She was a squeamish girl—she fled at the sight of cockroaches and spiders, and horror movies terrified her. And yet this odd creature, a monster by any definition, filled her with more love than disgust.

Was this the supposed 'maternal instinct' she had heard so much about? Jing had never expected to experience it. Especially not from a toyol!

Hafiz smiled. "This toyol seems extra pandai. Barely an hour old, and already can speak! Sure sangat mahal punya!"

"You can't sell him," Jing said.

"What?" Hafiz was stunned. Munira gasped. "Why not?"

"Because I am his mother," Jing said.

"Eh, jangan merepek, okay?" Ismail stepped forward. His face was red, and his nostrils flared. "We had a deal! This toyol is mine!"

"Okay, let's not get emotional," Dawn said quickly. "Don't shout, Encik Ismail. At this stage, the toyols are very sensitive to loud sounds. I'm sure that Jing doesn't mean what she said. It's the maternal bond kicking in. You know how mothers are."

Dawn attempted to rationalize, "Right now, Jing has just gone through a rather intense procedure, and her hormones are all crazy. Give her a while to settle down. Then she'll give you the toyol. All right?"

"No," Jing said. "This is my baby." She turned to Ismail. "I'm sorry. But I changed my mind. I'd like to keep it."

"Eh, babi! What are you trying to pull?" Ismail scowled. "Don't try and con me, okay! That toyol is mine!"

Munira whispered into Jing's ear. "What are you doing? Give it to them!"

"I'm sorry. But… I can't!" Jing shook her head.

"You promised this one to him," Munira whispered back. "It's not worth starting a fight." She squeezed Jing's hand tightly. "Come on," she said softly. "Say goodbye. Let's go home."

Jing was silent. She was being difficult, she knew. They had made a deal, that was true, and just an hour ago, she had wanted nothing to do with this.

But that was before she had seen the results. It was so unfair! If she had known she would have gotten so attached to this little creature, she might never have agreed to do this at all…

She hugged the toyol one more time, and kissed it gently on the forehead. It let out a chirp of delight.

"Goodbye, Bintang," Jing said. "Go to your new parents."

After that, Jing was given the opportunity to shower and change clothes. When she was done, Dawn escorted her and Munira down a few floors to a payment section, where she was met by a smiling Lewis.

"Hello, my girls!" he said. "How did everything go?"

"Seemed okay," Munira said. Jing was silent.

"Excellent," Lewis beamed. "Here is a certificate acknowledging you went through a registered toyol procedure at our center. The cost is covered completely by Encik Ismail and his wife, so no worries there."

He took out a bag with the Toyols 'R' Us logo on it.

"We've also thrown in some goodies for you. There's a free umbrella! And a catalog of all our products, including some of our upcoming ones. Use the code TOYOLTIME for a 15% discount on your next procedure!"

"Do you really think we'd go through all that again?" Munira's voice was icy, but Lewis either didn't notice, or didn't care.

"You never know what could happen!" Lewis said. "We also have a Friend Loyalty Program. Would you like to be a part of that?"

"Go to hell." Munira flipped him the bird. She and Jing walked to the exit.

"Don't forget, keep this place strictly confidential!" Lewis called out after them. "And thank you for using Toyols 'R' Us! Malaysia's No. 1 toyol production center!"

Outside, Ismail and Putri were standing by the road. Ismail pretended not to see them. His hands were in his pockets, and he was suddenly really engrossed by something he saw in the traffic.

Putri, on the other hand, smiled at the two girls.

"Hey," she said. "Thanks so much for helping us. I'm sure it must have been a lot for you."

"Yeah." Jing nodded. "I hope you treat him well."

"I will," Putri said.

A moment of silence. And then Jing piped up again. "Maybe I could come and see him, sometime?"

Putri frowned. Just as she was about to speak, however, a car pulled up in front of them.

"Time to go!" Ismail said. There was an urgency in his voice.

"I guess we will see," Putri said. Her husband took her by the hand, and pulled her into the car.

And then they sped off, leaving Munira and Jing on the street.

"Well, that was quite a day," Munira said. "You want to get dinner? I'll belanja."

Jing shook her head. "Actually, if you don't mind… I think I would like to go home."

There was a strange ache in her chest, and her heart was suddenly beating quickly. *Probably a little side effect from the surgery*, Jing thought to herself.

Or perhaps… it was something else?

# 10

## March 30, 8pm.
## Arun's Mamak, Bangsar.

Khairul always felt a little bit uneasy every time he went plainclothes. It felt like cheating.

He enjoyed the security and affirmation that a uniform brought; people knew who he was and minded their business, and he would mind his. There was an unspoken aura of respect and order that came with a uniform.

Now, however, in a normal T-shirt and jeans, he felt just like everyone else. Or so he thought. Could people tell? Was there something in his posture, perhaps? His speech, his gait, his restlessness, that might tick people off that he was a police officer? Was the 'cop' in him like a bad smell, remaining on him even after he took the uniform off?

He tried his best to look normal, act normal, as much as he could, knowing it was a losing battle. If you had to tell yourself to act normal, you were already failing.

His phone beeped: a notification from Routefinder. *You have just checked into: ARUN MAMAK.*

Khairul cursed. He really had to shut down that pesky app soon. As soon as he discovered how…

The place was half-empty. Customers were mostly students in uniform, or elderly men in shorts, eating briyani with their hands.

The delicious smell of curry wafted though the air. Khairul felt his mouth water.

Just then, he saw his contact sitting at a table next to the washroom. Fara Astaka, in a blue blouse and slacks.

A thought burst its way to the top of his mind: It wasn't too late to turn away. Was he doing the right thing, sharing information with this mysterious stranger? She was supposedly on his side, but how did he know for sure?

Khairul had thought about getting permission from his superiors to team up with Fara. That was technically the right thing to do.

In the end, he decided against it. He wasn't sure if Superintendent Leman had clearance to know about the Night Police or not. And he had a feeling that just mentioning the words 'toyol' or 'magic' in his presence would get him thrown out of the office.

Usually, Khairul worked alone. He preferred it that way, more freedom to follow his own instincts. And right now, his instincts were telling him to trust Fara. Something in her told him she could be trusted. She had helped with that toyol, after all…

*Oh well. What Superintendent Leman doesn't know, won't hurt him…*

"Inspector Khairul," Fara said as he approached the table. She did not smile. "So good to see you again."

"Same here," Khairul said as he took a seat. "Have you ordered already? The roti sardine here is the bomb!"

Fara shot him a look of disgust. "Please. I would never eat on the job. That would be unprofessional."

"Looks like it's just drinks then," Khairul said sheepishly, ordering a teh ais from a waiter that appeared right on cue. "So. How is everything?"

Fara nodded. "Good. How's your leg?"

Khairul winced. "It's okay. I'm walking a little funny, but I'll recover. Had to tell the doctor it was a dog bite."

"Good idea," Fara said. She lowered her voice. "They managed to get the toyol dispelled yesterday. My suspicions were right, it was under some kind of spell."

"A spell?" Khairul tried his best not to sound like a katak bawah tempurung. "What kind of spell?"

"We're not sure yet. We're still trying to identify the mana sources."

"Ah. So this mana, dari mana?"

Fara shot him a perplexed look, and Khairul hastily explained himself. "Sorry. It's a pun. I make them a lot."

"Humor is unprofessional and not encouraged, especially when it impedes investigation," Fara said. "Please don't make any more puns."

"Sadly, I can't completely guarantee that."

"Anyways," Fara ignored him and went on speaking. "It's hard for us to make things out. The spell casting sigils were very crude. Almost amateurish. But it's definitely a mind-altering charm. A powerful one."

Khairul shook his head. "I'm sorry, but this is still very hard for me to take. I mean, magic, bomohs… shit. I never believed in any of this."

"Well, believe it or not, magic is real and all around us," Fara said.

"Can I use it?" Khairul asked. "Or only certain people?"

"Anyone can use magic. But if you want to use it well, you have to train," Fara went on. "Most people go their whole lives without realizing they can use this gift. Which is good for the politicians. Most governments want to suppress the whole idea of magic."

"Why?"

"Because it's too dangerous," Fara said. "Can you imagine, if just anyone could cast a spell? If everyone realized they can blow up a building by just waving their hands? How would governments keep people in check? Our rallies are tense enough. Can you imagine if the protestors had magic? Or the police?"

"Didn't you tell me you were from Bukit Aman?" Khairul asked.

"Yeah. But we're not government. Or with the biasa police. Malaysian magic users have their own police force. Created and governed by us. Though we are really based in Bukit Aman. We try to be close as possible to the real police force, even though most of them don't realize we exist," said Fara.

Fara continued to explain, "Believe it or not, most major crimes in this country always have some kind of occult angle. From Mona Fandey to Sodomy I and II, there's always some bomoh pulling strings."

"I see," Khairul said. "So can *you* use magic, then?"

Fara shook her head. "Nope. To be honest, many of us in the Night Police try not to use magic at all. Most magic comes from dark rituals, or pacts with evil forces. There's always a danger of losing your soul. So we have the next best thing."

She took out her phone and put it on the table.

"Here. Check it out!"

Khairul picked up and examined what looked like a basic smartphone. Nothing out of the ordinary. Until he examined the display screen.

There, under the date and time display, was the word **SPELLCOM** in big block letters.

"This is a state-of-the-art spellphone," Fara said. "Made using a combination of magic and technology. It's got a lot of basic, common spells built into it."

"So, it's like a magic wand, then?" Khairul deduced.

"Yup. But one you can call people and take photos with. It's also a shitload more expensive."

She picked the phone up and fiddled with it, before aiming it at Khairul's glass of tea. To his amazement, the color of the liquid in the glass changed, going from a murky brown to bright red.

"Oh my God!" Khairul gasped. "That's amazing!"

"Don't be too impressed," Fara said. "It can only do very basic spells. Like what I just did? That's one of the most advanced spells in the whole database. And its only function is to change the color of your drink. It's a simple way to show people we're not lying, magic really does exist!"

"So what else can it do?" Khairul asked. "Your phone, I mean."

"Its main function is protection," Fara said. "Its Protector app shields me from magic. No one can cast anything on me. The phone also fires a minor disarming spell, reveals hidden things, and casts a scan shield. If I turn it on, anyone who looks at me feels sick."

"You used it yesterday!" Khairul exclaimed, remembering how ill he felt seeing her for the first time. "Shit, that's really cool."

"Drains the battery like mad, though." Fara shook her head. "I really don't understand. How come, even with all the advances in magic and technology, no one can make a smartphone battery that lasts for more than a day?"

"Anyway, I would *love* to give you a full run-through on the history of magic in Malaysia. But I suspect this toyol user is going to strike again soon. He or she is probably a rogue spellcaster of a high rank. I think he is catching toyols, and bewitching them to kill their owners."

"Their owners?" Khairul asked.

"Toyols are undead, so they have to be created or summoned," Fara said. "They are bound to an owner. They're the ones who tell it to steal things."

"So you're saying… all the dead people so far… they were toyol users?"

Fara nodded.

"How can we confirm? Is there a registry of toyol users or something?"

"No." Fara shook her head. "But I have a lead. Let's go meet my contact. She's one of the foremost experts in toyols in the country."

"Okay," Khairul said, finishing his drink. "I'll go get my car."

"Great," Fara said. "Can I get a lift?"

"You don't drive?"

"Nope. I have other ways of travelling."

"Oh," Khairul replied. "You fly on a broom?"

Fara shot him a disbelieving look. "No. I use Grab. Do you think this is *Harry Potter*? Can you imagine how idiotic I'd look, flying over the Federal Highway on a broom? And in the KL pollution! You want me to die?"

# 11

## March 30, 9.30pm.
## Carpathian Hotel, Jalan Bukit Bintang, Kuala Lumpur.

The traffic in Kuala Lumpur that night was, predictably, horrible. Rows of cars, lined up bumper to bumper, in a sea of red lights and honking. Even with their police siren, it took Khairul and Fara almost an hour to get from Bangsar to Jalan Bukit Bintang.

"Surely there has to be some kind of spell in that phone for this," Khairul grumbled.

"No magic in the world is powerful enough to stop KL traffic jams," Fara sighed.

The drive there felt like an eternity, especially since Fara did not want to answer any questions about her life. According to her, making small talk was unprofessional.

Khairul had a feeling that this was going to be a very long investigation.

They parked directly in front of the entrance of The Carpathian Hotel. "Benefits of being in a police car," Khairul explained, "you can park almost anywhere. Beats paying for a valet."

A doorman bowed as he let them into the hotel. Its entrance was richly decorated, there was a huge chandelier on the ceiling, and lush paintings were hanging above the reception. Next to that was a vast lounge, with red velvet carpeting. Guests in evening wear sat at mahogany tables sipping cocktails, while a Filipina singer in a red dress serenaded them with Sinatra.

"I've never heard of this hotel before," Khairul whispered as they made their way through the reception. He was suddenly conscious of how under-dressed he was. Damn, he really shouldn't have worn his torn jeans today.

"That's because it wasn't always a hotel," Fara said. "It used to be one of the residences of Tan Sri Ferdinand Ho."

"Damn. The real estate tycoon? I thought he lived in Hartamas."

"He used to live here. Now, he's converted it into a hotel. And his ex-wife still lives here. That's who we are going to see."

Khairul and Fara passed the lounge; the singer was now entertaining everyone with a slightly off-key rendition of "Colors of the Wind". They made their way to the lifts. Khairul whistled; the buttons were encrusted in gold plate. They were labeled from 'Basement' all the way to the 30th floor.

Fara, however, did not go for any of those. Instead, she took out her spellphone, and aimed it just above all the other buttons. After a few seconds, the end of her phone began to glow red, and a secret panel opened by the lift door, revealing another button.

The number '31' was written beside it in gold lettering.

"Holy shit!" Khairul was aghast. "How did you know that?"

"A lot of buildings have secret floors in them for magic users," Fara said. "You can access them through secret buttons in the elevators."

"Wow. That's up-lifting."

Fara groaned.

"Are you *seriously* a real policeman?"

When the lift doors opened, Khairul's first thought was that he was in a jungle of some sort.

The 31st floor was covered in greenery—not just potted plants, but actual trees and bushes sprouting from the floor, which was covered in actual grass. Tall angsana trees stood next to hibiscus bushes and banana trees, with various flowering shrubs blooming around them. Khairul recognized orchids, lilies, and bougainvilleas. The air was filled with the sound of birds, mostly the cawing of crows and the hooting of owls, combined with the rhythmic chirping of crickets. There was a strong smell of frangipani, so strong it almost made Khairul want to choke.

But this was impossible! How could trees grow on the top of a—

*Oh yeah,* Khairul suddenly recalled. *Magic.*

"Welcome to Viola Gardens," Fara said. "The Datin likes to spend her nights here."

And then, as if on cue, a small creature came up to them, running on all fours. Khairul resisted the urge to scream as he realized it was another toyol. It had the same huge eyes and green mottled skin as the last one he saw.

This one, however, wore more than a loincloth; instead, it had what appeared to be a dark blue porter's uniform. It smiled at them—showing a mouth full of fangs—and took a little bow.

"Fara," it said, in a voice that sounded like someone gargling with a mouth full of marbles.

"Hello, Alauddin," Fara said. "How are you?"

The creature gurgled again, before gesturing at them with its paw; it was obvious it wanted them to follow it. It then took off on all fours again, moving so fast it was almost cartoon-ish.

Alauddin led them to a grove of tall willows, all growing in a ring.

A long, rectangular table stood in the middle. And sitting at the head was a woman in a green kebaya. Her dark hair was tied up in a thick bun, a hairpin jutting through it like a skewer. She was slightly plump, and her large, intelligent eyes shone like diamonds in the middle of her lined face.

"Fara! So nice you could pop by, bitch!" She got up and embraced Fara, kissing her on both cheeks. "Can I get a smile?"

"No," Fara said.

The woman sighed. "I don't know why I even try." She turned to Khairul.

"Ah, this must be the new beau. A biasa! I like the looks of him already. Handsome. And fit! You must be a tiger in the bedroom!"

She winked at Khairul, and brushed his shoulder gently. An embarrassed Fara cleared her throat.

"Datin, this is Khairul. He's with PDRM, we're working together on a case. It's not what you think. At all."

"Really? Well, that's a pity," the Datin giggled. "A policeman, eh? A shame you didn't come in uniform. You know there's nothing I find juicier than a man in uniform. Except, of course, when he takes it off. If you know what I mean."

"Sorry lah Datin. We have to keep stoic at all times. Magical crimes are very serious matters," Fara said.

"Wouldn't kill you to let your hair down, once in a while. Or your pants!" The Datin slapped her forehead. "But oh! Look at me, going on and on and on. Where are my manners? Come, have some tea! I have a new canister fresh in from Nepal… God, you should try some! These Nepalese… I swear, if anyone could bottle an orgasm, it would be them."

She gestured at the table. "Just pull up a seat wherever you like. Don't worry about rank or status. We're all friends here!"

If Khairul thought this woman was unusual, she was nothing compared to her guests.

Four other toyol sat at the table. They were all roughly the same size, but that was where the similarities ended. Each looked so different from the other that a layman might have thought them all different species.

One wore an old-fashioned sailor suit with cap and jacket. The kind Donald Duck wore. His skin was not the sickening green that Khairul had seen on other toyol, but a creamy shade of brown.

Another was dressed as a cowboy, with denim jeans, a jacket and a wide-brimmed black hat. While his skin was green, his eyes were not as large and his features not as inhuman as the others. If not for the mouth filled with fangs, one could mistake him for a very small child at certain angles.

The third was in a Baju Melayu, with a black songkok and batik samping. His skin was a dark gray. Like the others, his ears were long and tapered. While the other toyols' ears pointed straight upwards, his were curved and protruded backwards, giving him an almost elven appearance.

The final toyol, however, was the most striking. It wore a frilly pink dress with a large bow at its back. A hat covered with red flowers sat atop a head full of brown curls. Its eyes were red and not quite as large as the others. It was… pretty, by toyol standards.

"Meet my dear little children! That's Gregory," the Datin pointed to the sailor, who grinned at them. "The cowboy is Jerome, and the other fellow is Hussain." She smiled as she turned to the toyol in the dress, who was clearly her favorite. "And this is little Melody."

Melody chirped and gurgled, rose from her seat, and went up to the Datin. The two embraced each other warmly.

"Now then," the Datin said, "let's get something to eat."

She clapped. To Khairul's amazement and horror, half-a-dozen toyol emerged from the trees around them. They were dressed in black waiters' uniforms, one carried a tray of cakes, another a teapot, another had plates of fine china.

And maybe it was just Khairul, but these toyol seemed more… bestial than the toyol seated at the table. All of them had snarling mouths, faces covered with scars, huge leering eyes and misshapen features, in contrast to the softer features of the Datin's 'children'.

Were they her actual children? Considering how toyol were made… Khairul decided he was better off not knowing.

The toyol waiters quickly set the table, moving with speed and grace. Plates, cups and trays were arranged delicately and precisely, not a centimeter out of place. Then they retreated into the shadows, disappearing so quickly it was as if they'd never been there.

Khairul noticed that while the cups in front of him were filled with tea, the cups in front of the toyols were filled with a thick red liquid. Again, he decided not to think about this.

"Try the Belgian waffles!" the Datin said happily. "Oh my god, they will make you *cream*! I got them from that new baker that just opened in Kenny Hills last month. You know the one? Next to the clinic?"

Both Fara and Khairul shook their heads.

"Well, you should really pay it a visit. Buns to die for." The Datin started to butter a scone. "Now then," she went on. "I know you never come to see me and the kids unless something is wrong. So tell me. What's the matter now?"

And Fara told her everything.

The Datin whistled. "Bodies? That's dreadful!"

She then shook her head.

"But I don't think it's the toyols you can blame, dear. Yes, I know they're a cute little bunch of bloodsuckers... but trust me, they usually drink very little blood at a time. A teaspoon or three. Otherwise, goodness, they'd drain my maids dry!"

*Makes sense*, Khairul thought. *Of course a rich and pampered character like the Datin would never stoop so low to feed the toyols herself. A shame, they might have enjoyed her aristocratic blood.*

"Well, Datin, something is doing that. And we did find this at the last crime scene," Fara said, handing her the flask containing the rogue toyol.

The Datin gazed at it deeply before holding it up, as if to examine it in the light. Then, to Khairul's horror, she opened its cover.

There was a fizz of gas escaping, and Khairul yelled as the creature shot out of the bottle with amazing speed. It landed on its feet, fangs bared and claws drawn. It shrieked—a sound similar to a car skidding—and leapt at the Datin...

… who quickly waved her arms, and shouted a foreign-sounding word. To Khairul's shock, the toyol began to grow bright red, and fell roughly onto the floor, as if hurled by an unseen force.

"Oh, dear little one, please don't cry," the Datin said, now on the fallen monster like a grandmother comforting a child's hurt knee. "Alauddin!" she shouted. "Get some bandages!"

She turned back to Khairul and Fara.

"This poor little toyol has been enchanted. See the red glow in its pupils? That's a Ferality Charm. Brings out the aggression in a person." The Datin smiled. "I remember my last husband, he would cast the spell on himself when we were in the gardens. Ooh. We used to have such tumbles. Rolling on the grass and clawing each other all naked. The best of times."

"Okay, a bit too much information, Datin," Fara said, and the old woman laughed.

"Someone here has turned this little teddy bear into a big old grizzly," the Datin said. She was now rubbing the back of the toyol; it was making little purring sounds of pleasure. "On humans, it makes them all savage for a while. Barely a few minutes. On toyols, the effects are more lasting. They're infants, after all."

"I also notice it only has one hand," Khairul said. "Does that mean anything?"

"I'm not sure. I don't think it was created like that," the Datin said. "Toyols are meant to steal, after all, and having only one hand would really handicap it. This was probably done to it deliberately. Maybe as a consequence of the spell on it."

"Aren't toyols immune to injuries by weapons?" Fara asked.

"Guns, yes. But knives… maybe not. No one has really tried to stab a toyol." She shrugged. "Why would you?"

"So who would do something like this?" Khairul asked.

"The Ferality Charm is quite rare," the Datin said. "The Education Magicsty removed them from textbooks a long time ago. For obvious reasons. But I can also sense the magic sigils on it... someone combined that charm with a Returning charm. So it makes the toyol go back to the person who summoned them, and then kills them."

The Datin continued to explain.

"The spell combination is really crude, it's almost painful. It makes me think we're dealing with an amateur spellcaster. Someone way out of his league for a spell of this caliber."

"You know anyone like that?" Khairul asked.

"I know a few people capable of casting a Ferality Charm, but I can't see any of them doing a thing like this. Then again, most of my friends are in the show toyol circle... we like our toyols as gentle as can be." She paused, before smiling. "But I know what you should do. You should look up my old buddy Lewis. Of Toyols 'R' Us."

"Toyols 'R' Us?" Fara was astonished. "Why the hell do you want us to go to that damn *mill*?"

The way she pronounced that last word, was in tones mostly reserved for more vulgar terms. Also with four letters. It was also a pleasant surprise, hearing the robotic Fara finally express some kind of emotion.

"Don't call it a mill, darling," the Datin said. "Me and Lewis, we don't always see eye to eye... but I have to admit, he is good at what he does. His company, it's no mill... why, it's a damn boutique. Look how good quality this toyol is! I'd bet my best two-headed dildo he's behind it."

The Datin dug into her handbag, and took out a business card.

"Here," she said. "This is his place. Getting in is, like, super tricky… it's closed up tighter than a nun's legs. But I'll tell you how. If anyone can help you on this case, it's Lewis. He can be a bit of a snob, but he's all right really."

# 12

## March 31, 10pm.
## Ismail's house, Kampung Attap.

"Well?" Putri demanded. Her arms were folded, and she tapped her foot restlessly.

"Sabar lah," Ismail hissed. "I'm trying to find the right part!"

He flipped through the *TOYOL INSTRUCTION MANUAL* in frustration. "History of Toyol… Warranty… Parts… Contact Address… celaka, where the hell is the beginning?" Did the font on these manuals have to be so damn small? Putri had conveniently misplaced her glasses, so it was up to him to read everything.

Ismail and Putri were both in their guestroom. It was the first time they would be using their toyol. Unfortunately, it was proving to be a little harder than expected.

He hated to say it, but he was having a bad case of second thoughts. Ismail was terrified of anything occult-related. His father had been a fire-and-brimstone imam, constantly terrifying his children how anything they did would immediately cause them to 'terjunam ke dalam bahang api NERAKA!'

Ismail feared for the sanctity of his mortal soul far more than his body. He never went to horror movies, and did everything he could not to be corrupted by the wiles of other religions. Ismail avoided certain food outlets (whose owners were known to be Jews), never ate hot dogs (their very association with dogs was too much for him), and stayed so far away from anything cross-shaped that Dracula would be proud. Would he be eternally damned for doing this? Ismail did not want to think about it. Instead, he visualized all the wealth he would be enjoying after this.

His hands were trembling as he finally found the relevant page. Putri made some tasteless joke about Parkinson's disease. Which he ignored, because he had no idea what that was.

"Starting In-vo-ca-tion," Ismail read. "Celaka, why must use so atas words? Step One. Remove the toyol canister from the box."

Putri rolled her eyes. "Kinda obvious, right?"

The canister was lighter than Ismail expected. He took it out of the box and placed it on the floor. Also inside were three little packets of uncooked rice.

"Step Two. Draw a circle on the floor. Blood is best, if not, chalk or paint will do," Ismail read.

He was secretly relieved to read this. Ismail was just as scared of blood as he was of the occult or other religions: just the thought of needles made him faint. This, he realized, made him a terrible candidate to be a toyol user. But it was too late for that now.

Neither Ismail nor Putri wanted to cut themselves, so they dug up some old watercolors. They drew the circle (more of a slightly squashed oval) on the floor.

"Step Three. Place the canister inside the circle. Open it and release the toyol."

Ismail took a deep breath. He took the canister and struggled to open it. Ten exhausting minutes of brute strength passed before Putri noticed a little button on the side, with **PRESS HERE TO OPEN** inscribed in red.

Ismail cursed, and did so.

Immediately, a slit at the top of the canister opened. There was a loud whirring noise as a glass cylinder slowly popped out of it. The cylinder's top was made of cork, and was filled with murky green liquid. There was an infant-like creature within; the star-shaped mark on its head was clearly visible even through the liquid and the glass.

Ismail and Putri looked at it in anticipation. Nothing, however, seemed to be happening. The creature was completely still.

*Well shit*, Ismail thought angrily. *Was this some sort of scam? Or did I get a defective one?*

"Eh, what the hell lah," Putri cursed. "Bangunlah, babi!"

Impatient, she tapped on the glass with one of her long fingernails; it was then that the creature stirred. Ismail and Putri gasped. The creature grinned, showing off a mouth full of tiny fangs. Immediately, it raised its tiny arm, knocking the cork top off the cylinder and onto the floor.

Tufts of smoke emerged out of the canister, and there was a hiss as the toyol climbed out, soaking wet. It walked to the outline of the circle and stopped, apparently unable to cross.

"What next?" Putri asked. Her face was white.

"I don't know," Ismail admitted.

His wife dug her nails into his arm, causing him to wince. "Read the manual lah, apa lagi?"

Ismail quickly picked it up and continued reading. "Step Four. Recite this in-vo-ca-tion, while scattering rice on the floor by the circle."

There was a small argument between Ismail and Putri about who would do what. They hurriedly came to a conclusion after the toyol, perhaps growing restless, begun to snarl.

Putri threw the rice on the floor, while her husband chanted, in a quavering voice:

*Bangkitlah hambaku!*
*Dengar seruanku*
*Ya beredarlah dari tempat ini*
*Dan buatkan aku kaya*
*Copyright Toyols 'R' Us 2019.*

"You don't need to read that last part lah!" an annoyed Putri chastised him.

Was that it? Ismail had expected some long, classical pantun. The damn thing didn't even rhyme! But the toyol had been completely still as he chanted. Its eyes glowed red as it appeared to take in every word.

"Once done, invite your toyol to go out and 'Make Master Happy'," Ismail continued reading. "Be kind to it. Assume you are talking to a small child."

"Okay," Putri said. She squatted in front of the toyol, and flashed it her biggest smile. "Go out and make ibu happy, okay? Find me lots of things."

She felt very stupid doing this. For a moment, it felt as if the toyol thought the same. It stared at Putri with a quizzical look in its big eyes. And then it nodded. The toyol took to all fours and ran out the circle, before leaping out through a tiny crack in the window.

"Now what?" a clearly terrified Putri asked.

"Step Five. Wait and enjoy." That was the final step in the book. And clearly, something easier said than done.

What followed was the most excruciating wait of Ismail's life.

Putri buried herself in a thick romance novel; Ismail parked himself on his couch and turned on the TV. Neither of them could really pay attention to what they were supposed to be doing.

*What would the toyol bring back?* Ismail wondered. *What if it brought back junk? Or something dangerous? Or cursed? What if it killed them? What if it was followed by the police? Or some sort of evil hantu? Or what if it didn't even come back at all???*

It was a restless night. Every loud sound was the toyol returning, every overheard voice the scream of a victim. Eventually, Ismail could take it no longer. He turned off the television and paced up and down the living room, until Putri screamed at him to stop, as it was super annoying. But he could not take his mind off the toyol.

Ismail sat on his favorite couch and bit his nails. He used to do this a lot, it helped him with anxiety. The last time he had done so, he was still a teenager. He then tried reading the newspaper, but this too was folly. Perhaps he shouldn't have started with the crime section. Every article with someone going to jail hit too close to home.

Putri, on the other hand, would walk to the guestroom every five minutes, to check if the toyol had returned.

"Kenapa lah lama sangat?" Ismail sighed. "Is this normal? We've been waiting the whole night!"

He cursed as his wife told him barely an hour had passed.

"Maybe we should talk to Harun," Putri suggested. "He can tell us what to expect?"

*Huh*, Ismail nodded. *That was actually a good idea.* If anything, it would pass the time for a couple of minutes. He took his phone and gave his cousin a video call.

Harun picked up almost immediately.

"Hello!" he sang into the phone. Harun was in a leather jacket and Black Sabbath T-shirt. "What's up?"

"Hi, baby!" Putri called out from behind Ismail. She was smiling widely. "How are you?"

"Good, good! Wah, banyak cantik malam ni!"

"We have a problem!" Ismail quickly interrupted, before the phone call devolved into an endless chain of flattery. "It's our toyol!"

He briefly explained to his cousin what they had just done.

His cousin laughed. "Adoi, why you so impatient lah? Give him time. Even DHL takes one day to deliver packages, okay? You think instant service? And the toyol is so small and cute. Of course he's going to take time!"

"But this long?" Ismail asked.

"Yeah lah. Like mine, sometimes I can wait, like, a night until he comes back. He needs time to find good stuff, kan?"

"So I should wait until tomorrow?" Ismail asked.

"No lah. You have a better model. Jasmin, right? I heard they are very fast. Give it two to three hours at least," Harun said. He yawned. "Anyways, I got to go now, okay? I'm at my friend's house, and we're getting ready to surprise him!"

"Talk soon, okay?" Putri called out. "Meet for brunch tomorrow?"

"Sorry, I have an early flight to Melbourne tomorrow!" Harun sang. "I'm gonna go home, pack, send Budin out for a while, and then get a bit of sleep. You know I just can't sleep on planes! Although it's gonna be First Class, baby!"

"So nice!" Ismail was envious.

"See you next time, okay? Or we meet in Melbourne! Soon you also can go on international holidays!"

Ismail hung up. He had no choice now but to wait.

It was 3am when Ismail heard a loud growl.

Putri had fallen asleep. Ismail had read every column in the paper at least six times (he was now a minor expert on Brexit and the Libyan civil war) and was now folding it into paper planes.

At the sound, he dropped everything. His heart thumping, Ismail rushed to the guestroom—and what he saw made him gasp.

The toyol was back. It stood in the middle of the circle, grinning. Each of his fingers had at least two rings on it. Its loincloth was stuffed with banknotes and trinkets and jewelry.

"Ya Allah!" Ismail exclaimed. He rushed to the toyol and started to pick at his haul. The worth of all the jewelry here was more than he made in a year!

The toyol looked at him with big, expectant eyes. It reminded Ismail of a puppy dog. It was as if it was saying, "Did I do good job, Master?"

Ismail patted the toyol on the head, and it gave out a loud chirp. It was almost cute.

Putri was delighted. "Amboi amboi amboi!" she exclaimed. "Big time ni!"

The manual came with a few phone numbers for a couple of brokers. Apparently, they could cash in their jewelry with them, at a charge of 10% of total value.

"Wah sayang," Putri smiled. "I really made the right decision lah, choosing this toyol."

She stroked Ismail's chest with her finger, a sly grin on her face. "Marilah, bang. Let's go and… celebrate."

"Celebrate?" Ismail was stunned. "You gila ke? What kind of place is open at this hour? We should… ohhhh!"

He could not finish his sentence. For his wife had literally pounced on him, planting a huge kiss on his lips.

Hot damn. She hadn't kissed him like that in *years.*

# 13

## April 1, 2.15am.
## Kuala Lumpur.

*Find money for Abah!*

That was the singular thought in Budin's mind as he scampered on all fours down the deserted street.

The street was dark, with only a single lamppost illuminating it. Only the most sharp-eyed would spot him; not that it really mattered. Because of the magic on him, and the unnatural speed he was moving, most people would only see a blur at foot level. They'd probably chalk it up to a rat or some other kind of vermin. Plenty of those here.

Suddenly, an overwhelmingly fragrant scent hit his nose, causing Budin to stop abruptly. There was something of great value in the area. He needed to retrieve it at all costs! Budin rose onto his hind legs and sniffed the air cautiously. He needed to get it, whatever it was!

He headed to the house the smell was coming from. To the human eye, it was a fancy bungalow with French windows, a huge gate, and a massive water feature in the garden. To Budin, it looked no different from any other house in the area.

Scaling the gate was easy. Budin then made his way through the garden. He scampered on all fours up a wall, and then shrunk himself to enter a tiny crack in the roof. It came as easy to him as breathing for humans.

From there, it was a matter of following his nose.

Budin ran through many rooms, all of which again looked the same to him. His previous experiences, however, had given him a rough idea of what some of them were for.

*This is where Abah would go to sleep*, Budin thought as he ran through a room with a huge bed.

*This is where Abah would go to eat*, Budin thought as he ran through a room with fruit piled in a basket on a table. They all smelled disgusting.

One room had an assortment of colorful toys. Budin was very distracted by a cloth elephant with huge ears, it was the cutest thing he had ever seen! The little toyol was tempted to stop for a while and play with it. Oh, what fun they would have, what adventures they would go on!

But no! Budin stopped himself. This was not what he was here for! Abah would be angry!

He would play later. Right now he had a mission!

After traversing two more rooms, Budin finally found the source of the smell.

It was coming from a ring, with a red jewel the size of a bottle cap.

This ring was currently on the finger of a portly, dark-skinned man sleeping on a large bed with green sheets. He snored very loudly. This almost deafened Budin, with his large ears and enhanced hearing.

This would be difficult. But not impossible. Budin had stolen stuff from tighter spots before. He hoped the man was not a light sleeper.

The toyol leapt on the bed. The sheets were incredibly soft, so soft that for a moment, Budin was tempted to curl up and take a nap too. But again, he reminded himself of his mission.

The man was still snoring as Budin crept up to him. Thankfully, his hand lay at his side, with the ring in plain view. The toyol carefully took hold of the ring and tugged hard.

Big mistake. The ring was tighter than expected. The man suddenly awoke, his eyes blazing. He screamed a swear word as he looked at his finger in shock. Budin hurriedly crouched behind one of the pillows.

When the man was satisfied all was fine, he went back to sleep. Budin hurried back to the finger. To his horror, the man suddenly turned over. Budin had to leap a foot in the air to avoid being crushed by his enormous girth.

*That was close! How embarrassing that would have been*, the toyol thought. Yes, he would have survived, but a man landing on him was like a car landing on a human. Getting free would have taken a lot of time and energy.

Budin went to the ring again and tried a different tactic. He slowly loosened the ring, turning it and inching it up the finger. This did not wake the man, although it seemed to give him pleasure; he laughed as Budin did it.

Finally, the ring was off! Budin wanted to sing in joy, but silenced himself. He placed his new treasure in his loincloth. Why humans wanted these shiny stones, he had no idea.

What the heck were they for? You couldn't eat them. You couldn't play with them. All they did was sit there and sparkle. Might as well wait for night and look at the stars, save your time. Give him a cloth elephant any day.

Budin left the house and made his way back to the street. It was less deserted now; people were exiting the night clubs nearby. Most were too drunk or preoccupied to notice a little toyol scampering at their feet.

He wondered what to do next. Should he go on another mission? This stone would already make his master very happy. Besides, it was already close to morning.

*Time to call it a night*, Budin thought. He sniffed the air again, picking up the faint scent of his master among a torrent of various other scents and fragrances. That would lead him home.

Fifteen minutes into his journey, however, he was suddenly aware of something unusual.

Carnival music!

Budin halted abruptly. The sound of an organ, pulsating through the air! He smiled as he danced to it, shaking his little arms and feet. This was magical!

As a general rule, toyols are sensitive to music, having super sensitive hearing and the impulses of an infant. But there was something different about this music. It was like nothing Budin had ever heard before. Its rhythm was intoxicating, one two, one two, one two three, a powerful charm that blocked out his senses and shut down his mind. It was the call of a siren, a pied piper's melody the toyol could do nothing about.

Budin forgot everything. He forgot his master, his mission, his nature. He gave in to the music, dancing as he scampered to the source.

X

The music led Budin into an old, rundown building in the middle of an overgrown park. Its floors were covered with grime, and there were drawings on its walls. The toyol noticed none of this as he danced merrily into the room where the music was coming from.

It was a clown.

He was turning the handle of an old-fashioned hand organ, from which the music emerged. There was a hat with a pretty flower on his head, and he wore a bright pink jumpsuit with over-large buttons. His face was painted white, and there were red stars around his eyes.

The clown smiled as he saw the toyol.

"Another one," he muttered as Budin approached, still dancing. "Another filthy abomination."

He bent over and grabbed Budin. Still caught up in the melody, the toyol did not resist, even smiling as the clown lifted him and began scrutinizing him.

"You dirty, foul creature," the clown said solemnly. "Scum of the womb."

There was a glint of light as he pulled something out of one of his jumpsuit pockets. Budin realized too late that it was a knife.

The toyol screeched as the clown suddenly struck, slicing off one of his hands with the knife. Blood gushed out into a puddle on the ground.

While they were undead, toyols still felt pain like any other creature. Budin was screaming in agony now, thrashing as he tried to get free of his captor's grip.

It was just then that the clown began to chant. He raised his other hand, and began making strange gestures.

His voice was low and somber. Within seconds, Budin's pain faded away, replaced by a cool, gentle tranquility that washed over his body in waves. The toyol stopped struggling, and started to smile.

The clown's chanting began to grow much louder, and soon it drowned out all other sounds. It rose to an overwhelming volume, like thunder, so loud it burnt Budin's ears.

And this made Budin's undead heart fill with fire. A red-hot rage overtook him, and the toyol was gripped with the uncontrollable urge to rip, to tear something asunder. His little limbs shook as he struggled to control the sensations within him.

The toyol's eyes turned red, and he unsheathed the claws on his single remaining hand. He screeched at the top of his little undead lungs. Why was he suddenly so… hungry?

And there was only one place to go.

The sound of glass breaking awoke Harun with a start.

"What the fuck?" he said, still groggy, unsure if this was real or some sort of weird dream.

*Burglars? Shit.* Thanks to his toyol, he did have a lot of wealth now.

Harun cursed. He should have known these toyols were too good to be true. Sooner or later, something like this was going to happen.

Still, he had always thought he would be taken down by the police. Not by a bloody burglar. Stupid karmic justice!

Well, it would not be so easy to take Harun down, that was sure. He picked up the baseball bat under his bed—he had started sleeping with one recently—and walked out of his room.

"Who's there?" he shouted. "I warn you, I am a black belt in karate!"

A lie. The closest thing he had to martial arts knowledge was watching every episode of *Cobra Kai* on Netflix. But the burglars didn't need to know that.

Harun gasped as he saw what was standing in the middle of his living room.

It was his toyol, Budin, surrounded by shards of broken glass. Behind him, one of the windows was broken.

*Oh!* Harun relaxed. It was just his toyol!

*That's weird. Didn't Budin usually come in without any trouble? And why hadn't it gone to the circle of rice?*

*Oh well. Maybe it made a mistake. Not like it could think. At the end of the day, it was just a dumb baby.*

"Oh, Budin! You gave me a heart attack!" Harun sighed. "Bad boy. Come to Abah!" He held out his arms and embraced his toyol as he ran up to him.

It was just then that he noticed there were a lot of things different about Budin.

His eyes—why were they suddenly red and glowing? Why were his claws outstretched? And why was there white spittle dripping out of Budin's mouth?

"Are you okay?" Harun asked. "What happened to your hand?"

And that was when Budin lunged at him, sinking his claws into the flesh of his leg.

Harun screamed and tried to run, but it was no use. He fell to the floor, his body overwhelmed by pain. Meanwhile the toyol had ripped off his sock with his teeth, and was aiming for Harun's big toe…

Ignoring his master's cries, Budin feasted like he had never had before.

# 14

## April 3, 2pm.
## Gerwaran Apartments, Subang.

"Jing?"

Jing opened her eyes. To her shock, Munira was peering over her, a look of concern on her face. "Are you all right?"

*What the hell?* Jing blinked several times, making sure this wasn't a dream. "How did you get in?"

"Your door was unlocked," Munira said sheepishly. She sat beside Jing on her bed. "I called you fourteen times, and you wouldn't answer!"

"I'm fine," Jing said. "I just wanted to sleep in today."

"And miss a class? Yeah, right," Munira snorted. "You have perfect attendance."

"Not any more."

Jing yawned, and sat up. She was wearing a blue blouse and jeans. Munira recognized it as the same outfit she had worn during their visit to Toyols 'R' Us. Her long hair, free of its usual ponytail, was tangled and coarse-looking.

Jing picked up her phone, and cursed to discover it was out of battery. "What time is it?"

"About two," Munira said.

"How did you find my place, anyway?"

"Asked Leong. I like what you've done with it, by the way."

"Oh please." Jing rolled her eyes. Her room had seen much better days. Her desk was covered with dust, and there was a heavy staleness in the air. Books and dirty clothes were scattered all over the floor. The wastepaper basket was almost overflowing with empty pizza boxes and beer cans. "Could you open the window?"

Munira did so, while Jing walked to the sink in the corner of her room. She began to retch.

"Good God!" Munira helped hold Jing's hair as she forcefully expelled the contents of her stomach. "You need a doctor!"

Jing shook her head. "I'm fine. Just a bit under the weather."

"What happened?" Munira asked.

"I dunno. I've just been so tired. I couldn't even eat lunch. I wanted to take a shower… but I didn't have the energy. I thought, what the hell, what does it all matter? I just wanted to curl into my bed and sleep forever."

"Shit," Munira said. "That sounds serious."

"Tell me about it," Jing said. "I'm a night owl. I usually don't sleep until two or three. But yesterday… all I wanted to do was sleep." She turned to Munira, and her voice was deathly serious. "Do you know what I dreamt of?"

"What?"

"My son. My toyol. His monstrous little face. He's a monster," Jing said, and her voice started to shake. "But I wanted him. I wanted him so bad. I wanted to hold him and cuddle him and love him. And I'll never ever get to do that."

"Oh my god," Munira said. "I think you're having a bad case of the baby blues."

"What's that?"

"My auntie had it," Munira said. "After she gave birth. She was very moody, and didn't want to eat or sleep for a few weeks.

Also cried a lot, sometimes for no reason at all. It's because of all the hormones, from the pregnancy and delivery." She held Jing's hand. "Although to be honest, I never thought anyone could feel that for a toyol."

"I know it sounds stupid," Jing said. "But I miss him. It's only been four days since I saw him. But it feels like fucking forever!"

She burst into tears, and Munira embraced her.

"I really fucked up," Jing said. "What do I do?"

"I don't know," Munira admitted. "But I don't think you fucked up at all. You were in a tough situation. I don't think there was any real 'right' answer there."

"I should have just kept the baby," Jing said. "Maybe that was the right answer. This is my punishment for giving him up."

Munira sighed. "You can't think that way."

"What kind of mother doesn't want her baby?" Jing's eyes watered again.

Munira took out a packet of tissues from her jeans and passed them to her friend.

"Look. You weren't ready for any of this. You didn't plan to have a fetus grow inside you. So you got rid of it before it could develop into a baby. It wasn't alive, not yet. There's nothing wrong in doing that."

"What if that baby were to become a doctor? Or the next Prime Minister, and a good one?"

"What if the baby were to be a serial killer? Or a cannibal? You can't make all these assumptions," Munira protested.

Jing laughed, despite her tears.

"I know it seems bad now," Munira said. "But don't worry, okay? I think you made the right decision." She sighed and took out a cigarette. "Is it OK if I smoke?"

"Yeah sure," Jing said.

Munira took a puff and put her hand on Jing's shoulder.

"Did you know I was abandoned as a baby?" she said calmly.

"Really?" Jing's eyes widened.

"My mum got knocked up by a guy she met in school," Munira said calmly. "He left her after she told him she was pregnant. Bastard."

"So your mother raised you by herself?"

"I wish," Munira sighed. "I said she abandoned me, remember? The pregnancy scared the hell out of her. She didn't know what to do. She didn't dare to go to the doctor, because the doctor was her mother's friend, and she was afraid her family would kill her if they knew what happened. She hid her pregnancy for months. Then, she gave birth to me at a toilet in a bus station. Left me in a shoebox, all covered in blood, and ran away. Luckily the cleaner found me."

She took a long puff of her cigarette.

"There was an article in *The Star*. The only time I'll make it to the newspapers."

"Shit. I'm so sorry," Jing said.

"Hey, don't be," Munira said. "In a way, I don't blame her. She was this poor 19-year-old girl with no idea what to do. Her family was unsupportive and her father wanted to disown her. If I were her, I'd want to get rid of me as soon as I could."

"I fucked up my mother's life. She was really smart, you know. Had a college scholarship, could have been the first in her family to go to university. Be a doctor. And then I came along."

"She dropped out of school. She couldn't afford the fees, and no one would support her. She had to go to jail for abandoning me. Came out a broken woman, and later had a sleeping pill overdose. She was only 24."

Jing turned pale. "I had no idea."

"I found this all out about three years ago. Tracked down my birth family. Luckily, one of my aunties would talk to me, although the rest pretend I don't exist," Munira said.

She sighed. "But you know the worst part? I managed to track down my birth father. At least I *think* he's my birth father, we don't have any official records, but everything matches up."

Her voice shook as she continued.

"That bastard is some big-time manager in a factory in Shah Alam. Doing very well. He started all this nonsense, and he got away scot-free!"

Jing shook her head. "That is awful."

"So, anyway," Munira said. "All this nonsense would have been avoided if two things had happened. One, my family had been supportive of my mother, instead of treating her like a bloody pariah. Two, if my mother had been able to abort her child properly. She was clearly not ready for a child, and it cost her life."

"But if she had the abortion," Jing said, "you wouldn't be here today."

"Yeah," Munira nodded. "But does that matter? I never asked to be born. And it's not like life has been great anyway."

She took another puff of her cigarette.

"My early years were rotten. Bouncing from one foster family to another. One was abusive. Another barely cared for me. I went through a lot of shit times, none of which I asked for. And it's not like my life is going to matter in the long run."

"Well, I'll say one thing," Jing said. "I am glad your mother did keep you. Because you've been so helpful, all through these crazy times."

"Awww," Munira laughed. "Well, aren't you sweet. But I guess what I'm trying to say is... a child is not always a blessing. Especially if you're not ready for it. You could have ended up like my mother. Her life cut short because of circumstances imposed upon her. For the last years of her life, she was broken and alone. I hope that never happens to you."

# 15

APR 3, 2.30PM.
TOYOLS 'R' US.

"Ah, this way ah, sir," Ah Chuan smiled. The old one-legged man led them to a waiting room with couches and a magazine rack. "You go the lift, then you go to top floor. Office is there."

"Thanks so much," Fara said.

"This is a really bizarre building," Khairul whispered to her. "Something strange is afoot. And I'm—"

'Inspector," Fara interrupted. "If you are about to make some kind of wordplay involving 'afoot' and that man we just met with only one leg, I am officially quitting this investigation!"

Khairul grumbled. "I wouldn't do that. That's kinda offensive. Shame on you for even thinking of that."

Fara rolled her eyes.

Getting to this place had been a nightmare. Finding an old building, putting in a keycode, finding a secret button… Khairul had gone to escape rooms which had been less complicated. How do you keep a place in business when you make it so hard for your customers to find you?

Khairul took out his phone and saved the location 'Toyols 'R' Us' under Routefinder. It was lucky that Datin Viola had given them exact directions. He and Fara could never have found this place on their own.

According to Fara, this place was commonly known as a toyol mill: It manufactured toyols for commercial purposes. Most mills, she told him, had been seedy hole-in-the wall outlets, nothing more than a single lab in a dusty room at a dilapidated shoplot. Toyols 'R' Us, however, had changed the game completely.

The company's rise had been covered in many occult tabloids ("There are occult *publications*?" Khairul had been stunned to know), and every bomoh in Kuala Lumpur knew its name.

Its rise was all to do with one man. Lewis Gnanasegaran, a pawang from Alor Setar. According to the stories, he was a restaurant owner in Sungai Buloh for four years until his business failed. One of his rivals had been using a toyol to secretly ferret away his money for years.

When Lewis found this out, his reaction surprised everyone. He was not angry or frustrated; legend has it he went up to his rival and shook his hand. "Such a little, ugly thing," he had said, seeing the toyol with his own eyes. "And this has been the cause of your wealth. Why didn't I think of this earlier?"

He enrolled in a business course. And two years later, he started Toyols 'R' Us.

It wasn't the first toyol mill, but it was the most advanced. Lewis updated this ancient trade, incorporating modern business techniques and cutting-edge scientific methods.

Customer loyalty campaigns. Designer toyol models. Toyol ownership packages for everyone from the common man to the aristocrat. Advanced toyol creation labs. Modern spellcasting techniques. Free umbrella with every purchase! Unsurprisingly, he became fabulously wealthy, with his name appearing regularly on *Misfortune Magazine*'s Top 10 Richest Malaysian Occultists lists.

One of his biggest successes had been to get toyol mills legalized. Before this, they were illegal and secret, whispered about in rumors. Due to their previous bad reputation, many of them had hid themselves, making people have to jump through various hoops to get to them.

Lewis introduced the idea that toyols could be used for good. Service toyols for the disabled were far more intelligent and mobile than dogs. Investigative toyols, using their powerful wealth-sniffing noses to find hidden drugs and contraband. Play toyols, to entertain children. Domestic toyols who could clean high places and crevices no one could reach.

Yes, it was argued, all this was well and good, but this was just a small proportion of toyol users. Most people still used them for crime.

*Ah*, Lewis reasoned. *Am I to be blamed for the criminal actions of my customers?* He gave stern warnings against using them for crime; was it his fault they wanted to proceed in that manner? If a man stabs someone, did you lock up the shop owner who sold him the knife?

Plus, he added, most toyols were easily countered. There were dozens of anti-toyol spells and charms that even a child could cast. Most magic users would not have to worry about them. The biggest group affected? The non-magic users, the biasa. And a lot of them were so much richer than your average bomoh or pawang. Read the biasa papers and you'd see articles about horrendous financial crimes involving obscene amounts of money. Wasn't it good to bring these fat cats down a peg or two?

Best of all, Lewis had more connections than Tinder. He knew kings and ministers and scientists and policy makers. A few honeyed words here, a favor there, a few palms greased and pockets filled, and toyol mills became legal in 2014. The only terms were that they had to maintain their secrecy, to limit the people using them—and pay a big fat licensing fee to the government every year.

Lewis was perfectly fine with these.

"Good afternoon to you, officers!" Lewis shook their hands as he welcomed them into his office. "How may I be of assistance?"

Lewis wore a crisp white suit, complete with handkerchief sticking out of his breast pocket. His office was spacious and brightly lit. A huge mahogany desk at one corner, next to several file cabinets and what appeared to be a hat rack. A furry rug next to two large chairs. Stacks and stacks of papers and folders on top of a coffee table.

A large oil painting was hanging on a wall, of a shirtless Lewis, his arms bulging with muscles, pinning a tiger to the ground.

"Art lovers eh? Excellent, great taste! I like you both already!" Lewis smiled as he noticed their interest. "That was me about 10 years ago. Kinda let myself go since then." He rubbed his stomach good-naturedly.

He took a seat behind his desk and faced the two police officers. "Now then. What seems to be the problem? I've been paying my taxes, keeping up with my special payments—"

"Oh no," Fara said before Khairul could say anything. "It's not you we need to talk about. It's about some of your toyols. I'm afraid they've been involved in some very… gruesome crimes."

Lewis gasped, perhaps a bit over-dramatically.

"My toyols? Impossible!" He shook his head. "My toyols are sweeter than gula Melaka! They wouldn't hurt a fly!"

"Well, we've had a toyol that drained its owner to death. Sucked up all his blood. And it's from your company, unfortunately."

"My toyols would never do a thing like that!" Lewis protested. While his voice was raised, his tone was still calm. Khairul was impressed that he was able to maintain his composure.

"We think someone has cast a Ferality Charm on them," Fara continued.

"Impossible." Lewis waved his hands dismissively. "Our toyols are 100% spellproof. We are in compliance with SIRIM and FARKIM certifications!"

"What do you mean?" Khairul asked.

Lewis stared at him with a look one would give a baby who had just soiled his pants. "My dear boy, all our toyols are marked with runes of anti-magic. Prevents people from enchanting or controlling a toyol that's already been summoned. We take quality control very seriously!"

"Is there a possibility this rune could be removed?" Khairul asked again.

"All our runes are top quality. Not even Mona Fandey herself could remove them!" Lewis said.

"Who is responsible for them?" Khairul asked.

"Our casters," Lewis said. "Down at the spellcraft department. I'll take you to them."

The spellcraft department was in the lowest floor of the building. At first glance, it looked very much like a science laboratory. Filled with men and women in lab coats doing science-y things with large beakers and test tubes. Inside their beakers, of course, were tiny humanoid fetuses with glowing eyes.

"These are new fetuses, obtained from a harvest team," Lewis said. "We place them in enchanted formaldehyde for about twenty minutes before our spellcraft team starts working on them."

They walked past a raised platform in the center of the room. It was covered by a pair of huge, heavy-looking metallic doors with large handles.

"This is Dr. Hafiz," Lewis said as they approached one of the scientists, who was dissecting the body of a tiny toyol. "He's deputy head of this division."

Hafiz smiled at them, and they all shook hands.

"These are Inspectors Khairul and Fara. They're investigating a crime involving a toyol," Lewis said. "Apparently one of our toyols has gone crazy, and has killed its master."

Hafiz looked shocked. "Eh. Tak mungkin kami punya!" He picked up the toyol body he was dissecting, and raised its right hand into the light. Something glittered—Khairul could make out a tiny, diamond-shaped mark of a silver steel-like material embedded in the toyol's palm.

"That's an anti-magic rune," Hafiz said. "No spell can affect it." He stepped backward. "Tengok."

Before Khairul could react, Hafiz took out his phone and waved it, muttering some foreign-sounding words. To their shock, a fireball emerged from its base. It zoomed toward the toyol, before exploding with smoke and a loud bang as it hit the creature. Khairul and Fara had to cover their eyes.

Once the smoke cleared, however, the toyol's body was completely unsinged.

"How come YOUR phone can't do that?" Khairul asked Fara, who merely shrugged.

"There you go," Lewis said. "The only magic that works on it is the magic that brought it to life. And the spell that keeps it bound to its master. Nothing else."

"The rune," Khairul said. "It's always on the toyol's right hand?"

"Ya, betul. That is our SOP. Although if we want, we can put it anywhere—"

"The toyol we captured had its right hand cut off!" Khairul said. "Would that remove the anti-magic effects on it?"

Hafiz looked at him in horror. "Ya. But why would you do that? That would make it hard for the toyol to steal anything! That's like you build a car, but throw away the front tire!"

Fara shook her head. "Mr. Lewis, I think someone is hijacking your toyols. And using them for dark purposes."

"But why?" Hafiz said. "Why go to all the trouble? Toyols are not built for killing. There are so many other creatures, bigger and more powerful. Ada pontianak… ada penanggal, ada langsuir… kenapa nak guna toyol?"

"That's what we need to find out," Fara said.

"These anti-magic runes," Khairul said. "Who puts them on the toyols?"

"Any of our toyol specialists. All normally supervised by the head of our department, Mr. Vellu. But since he's still on his kursus, I've been doing it. And before you ask, yes, I memang qualified!" Hafiz puffed.

"Why did—" Khairul wanted to ask, but he was interrupted by Lewis.

"What the hell do you mean Vellu's on a kursus?" Lewis said. His tone was dark.

"Isn't he? He said he was at a spellcasting kursus in Bangi!" Hafiz sputtered. "He's been sending reports since last week!"

"That kursus was last month! And it was only for two days!" Lewis was getting frustrated. "How long has he been gone?"

"A month, sir. I thought you sudah approve!"

"Can we see the office of this Vellu, please?" Khairul said. "Something tells me he might be the key to this whole thing."

Mr. Vellu's office turned out to be a dusty room filled mostly with bookshelves. It smelled heavily of sweat. Anatomical diagrams (mostly of infants) and motivational posters adorned its yellowing walls. There was a blackened apple core on a large desk; God knows how long it had been there.

"Maybe this is what kept the doctor away," Khairul quipped.

No one laughed. These toyol specialists were clearly a very serious bunch.

"He's a scientist, not a doctor," Fara sighed.

"And it was such a good joke setup too," Khairul shook his head.

Fara switched on her spellphone. It emitted a bright orange light, which she used to slowly comb every inch of the space.

Lewis shook his head. "I should have known. That bugger was dodgy as hell. Always taking extended leave, or misusing company resources! Should have fired him long ago."

"When did you last see him?" Khairul asked.

Lewis and Hafiz looked at each other blankly. "Tak ingat," Hafiz said. "We never really talked much. Nothing personal… it's just, he was our boss, you know? You never get too close to your boss."

Khairul looked through the files on a nearby shelf. Nothing too fancy, most of it sales orders and lab reports. The occasional leaflet for a biryani takeaway or a pizza restaurant.

"Hey," Fara suddenly exclaimed. "What's this?"

The orange light on her spellphone was flashing green near the wall behind Vellu's desk. Fara placed her palm on the wall, and a small panel opened.

Inside were several fifty ringgit notes, a packet of condoms, and six to seven thin slips of paper. These were all embossed with the logo for a 'Pandamaran Pits.' Each slip featured a printed row of columns, with handwritten words on them. *Mauler*, one said. *Ripper*, said another. *Crusher. Raksasa.*

Hafiz whistled. "Betting slips. For toyol-fighting pits."

"What?" Khairul looked baffled.

"Toyol-fighting pits used to be a popular pastime in the East Coast," Fara said calmly. "You enchant your toyol not for stealing, but for battle. Then you throw them together, watch them fight, and bet on the winner. Something like cock-fighting."

"Wow," Khairul said, his head spinning. This world was a lot crazier than he expected.

"Of course, toyol-fighting is illegal now. Most people think it's cruel," Fara went on. "Though that doesn't stop it from happening underground." She turned to Lewis and Hafiz. "Was Vellu a fan of toyol-fighting?"

Lewis looked baffled. Hafiz, on the other hand, turned an odd shade of red. It didn't take Khairul's policeman's instincts to guess that he was clearly hiding something.

"Hafiz," he said, slightly sternly. "What do you know about this?"

"Vellu was a big fan!" the man suddenly burst out. He looked as if he was about to cry. "He went there every week. He said he had a lot of debts to pay."

"Really?" Lewis was shocked. "He didn't go under the company name, I hope?"

Hafiz shrugged.

"With company toyols?"

Hafiz hung his head. "Yes. He would breed some to be fighters and bring them there. Apparently he did quite well. Menang banyak."

"Bastard! That is absolutely forbidden! Misuse of company property, engagement in illegal activity," Lewis fumed. "Did he ever contribute any of his winnings to the company?"

Hafiz shook his head, and Lewis looked like he was about to explode. "My god, when he gets back, there will be hell to pay!"

The rest of the investigation went smoothly. It took a bit of persuasion, but Lewis agreed to cross-reference the names of the previous murder victims against the company's list of clients, to confirm if they had purchased toyols from them.

The two investigators thanked the Toyols 'R' Us employees for their time, and headed out of the lab. Again, they passed the raised platform in the middle of the room.

"What exactly is that, anyway?" Fara asked.

"It looks like a trapdoor," Khairul said. It looked like it could easily fit a large man. "Is this some sort of escape hatch?"

"Oh no, bukan," Hafiz smiled. "It's a disposal hatch. We throw all our failed experiments down there."

There was a groan from Lewis. Hafiz immediately stiffened, suddenly aware he had said the wrong thing.

"Failed experiments?" Fara was stunned. "As in, toyols that don't meet your quality standards? That is a crime! Illegal disposal of supernatural creations!"

"What exactly constitutes a 'failed experiment'?" Khairul asked, and Hafiz turned a bright shade of red.

"Look, there is clearly a misunderstanding," Lewis smiled. He flashed a dark gaze at Hafiz. "I'm sure everything is accounted for."

"We will look into this later." Fara shook her head. "It's lucky we have more important things to do now. But you better have a damn good excuse next time we see you."

"Toyol-fighting is filled to the gills with unsavory characters," Fara said as they walked back to their car. "Maybe this Vellu pissed off the wrong guy, and they decided to take revenge?"

"Maybe," Khairul said. "I'll look up Vellu's details in our database. Although something tells me he isn't going to be found very easily."

"I think our best bet is the toyol-fighting pits," Fara said. "Flyers say the next event is this Friday."

"I've always wanted to go to Klang." Khairul smiled.

Just then, his phone rang. It was Jairuz.

Khairul told Fara to wait in the car, and picked it up.

"Eh, boss," Jairuz said cheerily. "Free to talk?"

"Yup. What's up?"

"Another body found. Same method of death."

"Really?"

"Yeah. Helen Ambinata, 43, Bangsar. Body completely drained of blood, wound in big toe. Nothing stolen, no sign of a break in. The usual lah."

*Shit,* Khairul thought. *Another death, which we had failed to stop.*

Khairul suddenly felt nauseous. Memories of the previous serial killer case forced themselves back into the forefront of his memory. He knew he could not go through all that again.

"Jairuz," Khairul said. "I need you to try something. Have you searched the house already?"

"Ya. But I haven't found any—"

"Search again. And this time, look for a canister filled with liquid. Maybe about seven inches high, yellow in color. There might be some kind of creature inside."

"*What?*"

"Yes, you heard me correctly. Go look for that. Look in cupboards, shelves, wherever!"

"Apa tu?" Jairuz was completely confused, it was almost cute. "You're sure I'll find one?"

"I don't know," Khairul admitted. "But if you do, it'll be a huge lead."

He hung up, and walked back to Fara, who was standing outside the car. She held a lit cigarette.

"All good?" she asked.

"There's been another murder," Khairul said. "Oh shit, sorry I forgot to unlock the car."

He did, and the two stepped inside the squad car.

Just then, there was the sound of a chime: a WhatsApp message from Jairuz, together with an attached photo.

His message simply read:

How did you kno???

# 16

## April 5, 9pm.
## Pandamaran Fighting Pits, Klang.

Khairul had no idea there were so many secret places in Malaysia.

His mind boggled. First they had gone to a hidden floor in a swanky hotel in Kuala Lumpur. Two days ago, they went to a secret toyol company in an abandoned building. And now they had driven to the outskirts of Klang, to find a fighting pit for the undead.

Khairul rarely came to Klang. After all, the most famous thing about the place was bak kut teh: a pork soup dish which he couldn't eat because of his religion. And the second most famous thing? Gangsters. Klang was a crime haven, the haunt of many of the most dangerous gangs in Malaysia. Most cities had a criminal underbelly; in Klang, it was the whole stomach, torso and head.

The journey took almost an hour. Rather than face another silent journey there, Khairul decided to turn on the radio.

"I don't think we should be doing that," Fara protested. "Music is—"

"Unprofessional? Relax, I won't tell your boss if you don't tell mine," Khairul said.

He activated his car's Bluetooth speakers, and a familiar tune began playing.

"Dear God," Fara's eyes widened. "Isn't this…you can't be serious!"

"Baby Shark!" Khairul replied, a huge grin on his face. "It's part of my 'Don't Fall Asleep!' playlist."

Seeing Fara's baffled face, he continued.

"I used to have a lot of night cases. Late night stakeouts, that sort of thing. So I compiled a collection of songs to help me stay awake no matter how sleepy I got. Most of them are extremely annoying or catchy. The Macarena, Crazy Frog, the Spongebob theme song, Friday, most of the songs of Justin Bieber…"

"You cannot be for real!"

"Hey, it works. And it's a lot cheaper than coffee."

"I'd rather tear out my ears then keep listening to this! God, is that song *repeating itself*?"

"It's on loop! Doubles as an interrogation method. Most suspects would rather sing like canaries than spend fifteen minutes listening to this."

'Baby Shark' had ended, and now it was on to 'Who Let the Dogs Out.' Khairul insisted on singing along to the whole thing, barks included.

"Do you ever take *anything* seriously?" Fara shook her head. "Is everything just a big joke to you?"

"Life is crazy," Khairul said. "If you don't laugh at it, you'll go mad."

X

The coordinates on the flyer led them to what looked like an old abandoned warehouse (Khairul promptly saved it in Routefinder as 'Toyol-fighting Pits'). It was a large brown building, with a pointed roof. About two dozen cars were parked around it, although no one could be seen in the vicinity—a major sign something fishy was going on.

"Now what?" Fara asked.

"Let's go in," Khairul said as he parked.

"If anyone asks, we're from out of town," Fara said. "Our friend Vellu told us about this place, and we wanted to make some bets."

"THAT is the cover story you come up with? Boring! Why can't we be international toyol smugglers? Or talent scouts, looking for the next big toyol TV star?"

"The simpler the backstory, the better."

"Okay. How do we know each other?"

"Ah," Fara said. "We're… brother and sister?"

"That will never work!" Khairul exclaimed. "We look nothing alike!"

"People won't question that!"

"Why don't we say we're a couple instead?"

Fara paused. "I guess we could."

Khairul burst into laughter. "Oh my god. Are you *blushing*?"

So, Special Investigator Fara Astaka was capable of regular emotions! This was quite a relief. Khairul hadn't been sure if she was truly human, or some kind of magical emotionless avatar, summoned into existence to combat the forces of evil.

Damn. That actually sounded pretty cool. Probably the premise of an anime. But ah well. Having a partner that wasn't a stoic robot was also pretty good.

The old man at the door stared suspiciously at them. His face was lined with wrinkles, and his gray mustache was so thick, it almost covered his entire upper lip.

"Who are you again?" he asked in Cantonese.

"My name is Megat," Khairul smiled. Years spent studying in a Subang college had given him a rudimentary grasp of the dialect. "And this is my… cousin, Laila."

Fara nodded, slightly reluctantly.

The old warehouse was almost deserted. Khairul and Fara entered through a pair of huge metal doors, which creaked ominously as they were pushed open. The place was dark; both Khairul and Fara had to turn on the lights on their phones. There, they found themselves in a huge hall full of dusty, rusted machines, which included a disused crane and cement mixer. Old cans and cardboard boxes were littered all around the grimy floor, and an overwhelming stench of decay hung in the air.

A small bit of exploring revealed a small corridor leading to a red door. It opened to this old man, manning a small booth outside another door.

"Why are you here?" the old man asked. He was carrying a torchlight, which he waved at them accusingly like a knife. Khairul wondered how long he had been sitting in the darkness.

"The toyol-fighting. Our friend Vellu told us about it. Do you know him?" Khairul asked.

The man sneered. "Ma chao hai, you think I know everyone here is it?"

"Sorry. Just asking. Who runs the fights?"

The man ignored him. "12 ringgit each," he said. "You go counter get your slips. Five fights tonight. RM50 minimum."

He insisted on giving them a light body search; Khairul had anticipated this and not brought his gun. He wanted to insist Fara not be subjected to it, but his partner shot him a look saying 'it's fine', and went along with it.

After that, the old man waved them through, and Khairul and Fara stepped through the door into the Pandamaran Toyol-fighting Pits.

X

Whoever called this place the fighting pits, they certainly weren't kidding.

It was a hall with a massive hole in the floor. Probably an empty swimming pool. The hole was about six feet deep, layered over with cement, with two large circles drawn in red paint. Everything was bathed in dim red and blue lighting. Neon lights shaped like Chinese characters crackled from the walls. The overwhelming fragrance of cigarette smoke wafted through the air.

People were seated at red plastic tables all around the pit. They were all men, with the majority Chinese and middle-aged. Most were casually dressed in T-shirts and jeans, although one table featured seven men in suits and sunglasses. Everyone was chatting loudly and drinking; pretty girls in very low-cut cheongsams walked around pouring jugs of stout. None of the girls looked older than 20.

A man was polishing glasses at a small bar opposite the entrance. A painting of the head of a black goat hung above him. The two headed there, ignoring the whistles and lecherous leers cast at Fara by the crowd.

"Hi there," Khairul greeted the bartender as he and Fara sat down. "Could you get me a Coke? And for her—"

"A Jagerbomb please," Fara said.

The bartender smiled. "Boleh ke, puan? Nanti kena tangkap oh!"

"Kami masuk lokap sama-sama," Fara winked at him. "Seronok kan?"

The bartender laughed, sounding like a horse choking. He started to pour drinks.

"How's the toyol-fighting here?" Khairul asked as the bartender served them. "Any tips?"

"New here, is it?" the bartender asked, and Khairul nodded.

"There's a lot of good choices," the bartender said. "Ripper is a good bet. Lao Lao also wins a lot. His claws are very sharp. Just don't bet on Emperor. He damn sui one."

"Thanks. By the way, do you know a friend of mine? His name is Vellu. He recommended me here."

The bartender laughed again. "Aiyo! That sorchai ah? Friend! He's in a lot of trouble."

"What kind of trouble?"

"I don't know lah. I meet so many people, cannot remember everything." The bartender winked at Khairul. "But dunno lah. Maybe you have something that can help me remember."

Khairul sighed. He was familiar with this song and dance routine.

He took RM50 out of his wallet (*that was this month's Netflix payment*, he thought bitterly) and passed it to the bartender.

The bartender gave an exaggerated gasp— he would have made a terrific actor— and struck his head with his palm. "Oh ya, now I remember. Tall guy, right? Beard?"

"What do you know about him?" Fara asked.

"That fella ah, got problem wan. Seriously addicted. He come in, bet thousands of ringgit. But he damn sui. Almost always lose. One time I think he lost one million. Chisin!"

The bartender picked up another glass and began to polish it.

"He borrow a lot of money from Ah Long. Idiot. Own money cannot win, want to use other people's. Cannot lah. Of course he couldn't pay back. They went to his house and caught him. Whack him kao kao, he ran away."

"So, you mean he's gone?" Fara asked.

The bartender laughed. "Hah. He should have. But no. He likes this place too much lah."

He paused a while for dramatic effect, before continuing. "So he change his face. Cut his beard. Change his hair. So now no one can recognize him."

"Where is he now?" Khairul asked.

The bartender's eyes glimmered. "Aiyah. I cannot remember lah. But maybe—"

"Oh for God's sake," Fara cursed.

Before anyone could say anything, she grabbed the bartender's arm. She forced it down onto the table, twisting it hard; the bartender yelped in agony.

"I'll ask you one last time," Fara said. "Where. Is. Vellu?"

"Please....stop." There were tears in the bartender's eyes. All around him, everyone was caught up in their own worlds. None of them noticed or cared about them. "I..don't..know...where."

"Not good enough," Fara said. She pushed harder on the bartender's pinned arm, until he finally squealed.

"Watch tonight's fight! He's there! Please lah, LET ME GO!"

Khairul took a seat at an empty table, while Fara waited for an order of potato wedges. A sort of thank you to the bartender for his last tip, and in a way, an apology for almost breaking his arm.

The seven men in suits were at the table beside him. They all had copper brown hair, styled and gelled to the point they almost resembled anime characters. All were rail-thin, except for one, who had a lined face and pot belly; Khairul assumed this was their leader.

He sipped his drink, while taking in his surroundings. Everyone around him was still chatting raucously.

Just then, Fara reappeared, snacks in hand.

"Good view," she commented.

Khairul munched on a potato wedge. "A place like this… is it legal?"

"It could be," Fara said. "But you need a license from the local council. And I'd bet my ass this place doesn't have one."

"You don't want a potato wedge?"

"I don't eat on the job, remember? Unprofessional."

"But strong-arming that bartender wasn't?" There was genuine admiration in Khairul's voice. "Where did you learn to do that?"

"I told you. I don't do small talk."

Khairul considered pressing further, but ultimately decided not to. After all, he had just seen what Fara was capable of doing.

Just then, the lights went out, and a spotlight shone into the middle of the pit. Loud applause filled the air as everyone averted their attention there.

A woman dressed in a very provocatively cut pink blouse and short shorts was standing there, a microphone in hand. A red cloth was wound around her right arm.

"Ladies and gentlemen, welcome to the Pandamaran Toyol-Fighting Pits!" she announced cheerfully, before abruptly switching to Cantonese. "My name is Shu Lin, and thanks for coming! Wah wah, we have another exciting night for you! Ten of the best toyol fighters from all around the country, gathered for an unforgettable fight! Are you all ready to win some money!?"

The crowd cheered.

Shu Lin went on a bit about betting procedures and minimum bets for a while, before announcing the first match.

"Okay, everyone!" she said excitedly. "Coming all the way from Raub, Johor… a three-time Toyol Ultimate Champion winner… with his unbelievable Razor Claw! Please give it up for Genghis, and his master, Kaduk!"

Loud applause and whoops. A door on the right side of the pit's wall opened, and the spotlight shone on a man walking through. He wore jeans and a backward turned baseball cap.

The crowd was not cheering for him, but for a small creature by his side. Another toyol… this one, however, was slightly larger than the ones he had seen at Datin Viola's. Like the rest, it looked like a misshapen baby in a loincloth. This toyol, however, had long steel claws strapped to his tiny arms, and golden spurs attached to its ankles. Its already not-too-handsome face was covered with scratches.

The two stood in the middle of one of the circles drawn on the floor. "BLOOD!" the smartly-dressed men beside Khairul were screaming. "WE CHOOSE YOU! GENGHIS! DON'T LET US DOWN!" Everywhere else, people were pounding on tables and whistling.

"Give it up one more time for Genghis!" Shu Lin announced. "And now, his opponent… a newcomer in the scene, but with an incomparable fighting spirit… please welcome, a new challenger, Hammerhead! With his master, Sivalingam!"

Applause, not as loud as before. A man and toyol stepped out of a door at the left of the pit. The toyol was large, with leathery skin and tufts of green hair on its head. It smiled, revealing rows of red-tipped fangs.

This time, it was not the toyol that had Khairul and Fara's attention, but its master.

"Shit," Fara said. "Is that who I think it is?"

Hammerhead's master was a tall, dark-skinned man in a smart button-down shirt and white slacks. He had shaved off his beard and mustache, grown his hair long and dyed it silver. But there was no mistaking his distinct features. Fara and Khairul had seen a photo of him barely an hour ago.

He may have been calling himself Sivalingam, but this was unmistakably Vellu, the missing scientist from Toyols 'R' Us.

'Sivalingam' stared at the audience blankly as he and his toyol stepped into the arena. Kaduk stuck out his tongue at them, an act which earned loud cheers.

"Oh wow, real mature." Fara rolled her eyes.

"Let's have a good fight, okay? Let the blood fly!" Shu Lin chirped happily. She raised her red cloth into the air. "Now, get ready to…… FIGHT!!!!"

Shu Lin stepped out of the ring. A loud airhorn sounded, causing Fara and Khairul to cover their ears. Everyone else cheered as the two toyols ran toward each other.

Khairul was immediately taken by how ugly and brutal it was. Both toyols fought mainly with their claws, jabbing with great speed. Bits of flesh and greenish blood flew into the air with each jab; the toyols, however, didn't show any pain.

Hammerhead was bigger and held its ground, but Genghis was faster and more savage. And those steel claws it had were deadly; the crowd ooh-ed every time it sliced off a little more of Hammerhead's flesh.

Behind them, their masters were barking commands. It was hard to hear them over the crowd's applause.

"AIM FOR THE THROAT!" Vellu was shouting.

"RIP HIM TO SHREDS!" his counterpart bellowed. "USE YOUR TOMBSTONE KICK!"

The crowd gasped as Hammerhead suddenly rushed at its opponent, knocking it down with the sheer force of its weight. Genghis was sprawled on the floor, taken completely by surprise, and Hammerhead walked toward it, snarling like a hungry lion.

The crowd's shock turned to cheers, as it turned out Genghis was only faking. As Hammerhead approached, it sprung up like a grasshopper. It lashed out with a powerful claw, slicing off one of Hammerhead's eyes. Torrents of blood splattered on the floor. Hammerhead gave a screech of pain. Behind him, his master cried in shock.

All this violence was enough to make Khairul queasy. He turned away as Genghis shrieked in triumph and headed toward its fallen foe. Fara, however, kept watching, her face as impassive as ever.

"FINISH HIM!" the guys at the table next to Khairul were cheering. "FINISH HIM!" Their leader was grinning like a fool.

And for a moment, it looked as if that was going to happen. Genghis lunged at Hammerhead, which was still reeling in agony. Hammerhead, however, anticipated this attack. The toyol grabbed its opponent's outstretched claw, ignoring the agony as the metal edges cut into its skin. Using all its strength, it pulled Genghis to the ground. Then, in one final attack, Hammerhead lunged forward. It opened its large jaws, its yellow teeth glinting in the spotlight. It bit hard into the back of Genghis's neck, and tore its throat out.

Chaos erupted. Both boos and cheers rang into the air.

"UNFAIR!" the men at the table next to Khairul were screaming as Genghis's body slumped to the floor. "CHEATING! CHEATING!"

In the arena, Kaduk was throwing a tantrum, cursing at the people at the tables nearest to him. Hammerhead collapsed in exhaustion, while its master was grinning from ear to ear.

Shu Lin stepped back into the arena. She picked up the tiny toyol's paw, and raised it triumphantly.

"THE WINNER!!!" she exclaimed.

There would now be a 15-minute break. The next match would be a cage match; some champion from Indonesia was involved.

Khairul and Fara had seen enough toyol-fighting to last their entire lives. They left the tables, heading to the club's backstage area. According to the bartender, that was where the champions waited in between matches. Normally outsiders weren't allowed in, but he could make special arrangements.

Khairul and Fara found themselves in a dimly-lit room filled with plastic chairs and tables. The floors were wooden and dusty, and posters of Cantopop stars hung on the walls.

Vellu was standing by the entrance. He was holding a large jar filled with dark fluid; even from afar, it was easy to make out the shape of a creature within. The man was speaking to a young girl behind a counter. There was a large machine beside her. It resembled a cross between a vending machine and a pipe organ.

"Welcome to our toyol center," the girl chirped. She looked to be in her late teens, in a low cut-cheongsam and bright pink hair. "We restore your injured toyol to full health! Would you like to rest your toyol?"

"Damn right," Vellu muttered. He handed the jar over to her.

The girl moved over to the large machine. She placed the toyol jar into a slot at its front, and activated a lever. The jar began to vibrate and glow blue.

"It should take about a minute," the girl said. "It's treating Genghis first. The injuries your toyol inflicted were very severe."

"I'd say," Vellu said. "Hey, can I buy you a drink?"

This was Khairul and Fara's cue. They stepped up to him, badges at the ready.

"Excuse me, sir." Khairul tapped him on the shoulder. "Vellu Jeganathan, right?"

Vellu froze, it was almost comical. To his credit, he recovered his composure quickly.

"I'm sorry, you've got the wrong guy." The man shook his head.

"Can it," Fara snapped. "We need you to answer a few questions. Please—"

"Fuck off," Vellu snapped. He tried to walk away, but Khairul grabbed his arm.

"Maybe my friend didn't make herself clear," Khairul said, as Vellu glowered at him. "You're being summoned for a murder investigation under section—"

"Murder investigation?" Vellu's eyebrows raised. "Shit, I didn't know that. All right, I'll come with you. But can I just get my toyols first?"

"All right. But make it fast," Fara said as Khairul loosened his grip. Vellu glared at her, before turning to the girl at the counter.

"Thanks for using the toyol center!" the girl chirped as she handed Vellu his jar. "Your toyol is fully healed. We hope to see you again!"

"Thanks," Vellu said. He opened it and peered inside, as if to check on the contents. Then, without any warning, he threw the jar to the floor. Khairul and Fara had barely enough time to leap away. The jar shattered into pieces, and Hammerhead the toyol emerged, his eyes glowing red.

"Rip them to shreds!" Vellu cried, before running toward the door.

"Celaka!" Khairul cried. He wanted to give chase, but Hammerhead had leapt on him. He screamed as the tiny toyol slashed viciously at him with its tiny but sharp claws, drawing blood and sending tiny chunks of flesh flying into the air.

Fara picked up a nearby chair. The girl at the counter screamed as Fara swung it at Hammerhead with full force, knocking the toyol into the nearby wall with a huge 'thunk'.

"Let's go." Fara helped her fallen partner up. Khairul struggled to stand, but the agony in his leg was too much, it was still bleeding profusely.

"The same damn leg," Khairul cursed. "Don't worry about me. Go get him.."

Fara nodded. She ran out the door.

"And call for backup!" Khairul called after her. He staggered to another chair nearby and sat down. The girl at the counter stared at him, fear in her huge eyes. Khairul asked her to get some bandages and iodine.

As he did his best to elevate his leg, he heard some snarls. In the corner of the room, Hammerhead had recovered, and was now running toward him on all fours.

Khairul instinctively reached for his gun, only to recall he had not brought it. He leapt off his chair as the toyol sprang at him. It collided with the wooden counter and collapsed in a half-daze.

Khairul picked up his chair.

"Well, Hammerhead…looks like you've just been *nailed*."

With that, he swung the chair as hard as he could. It broke into bits as it collided with the toyol, knocking it out cold.

"Oh my God," the girl from earlier had returned. She was wide-eyed and applauding. "That was so cool!"

Someone had overheard his badass one liner! This was a very good night indeed.

Meanwhile, Vellu had made his way out of the fighting pits, and was rushing to the parking lot. He needed to get to his MyVi, and get the hell out of here.

*Fuck it,* he cursed. *How did the fucking cops get involved? I covered all of my tracks…*

And he had been doing so well, too. Vellu recently managed to pay off two loan sharks. Hammerhead was fighting at his peak, and his other toyols were also doing well. If they kept up their winning streak, he would be out of debt in three or four years. Then he could start afresh: restart the toyol-fighting, this time with a proper strategy, no more going in blindly…

But what could he do now? His only option was to lie low. Run to Thailand for a while, perhaps. Change his name, wait for a month until things quieted down. Earn an honest living for a while, as horrible as that may be.

Vellu wove his way round the rows of cars, peering around cautiously. Thank goodness there was no one around. He had given those cops the slip.

*Who ratted me out? One of my colleagues back at Toyols 'R' Us? Stupid idiots. I should never have gone to that place to begin with.*

*Or maybe... it was that asshole from last month. The bloody zealot.*

He knew it had been a mistake to talk to him from the beginning. But why would he rat him out? It didn't make any sense!

Just then, a man emerged from the shadows. He had copper hair, and was wearing a smartly-pressed suit. "Excuse me, sir," he said in a very heavy Chinese accent. "Mr. Vellu Jeganathan?"

Vellu cursed. This was seriously not his night.

"No, you got the wrong person," he said. He stepped away carefully; however, another guy, also with copper brown hair, stepped out from his left. Vellu turned, only to face another guy; soon, he realized he was surrounded by six or seven of them.

"Fuck," Vellu said.

"Mr. Vellu," one of them said. He was the portliest and oldest of the gang. "Damn brave ah you, coming back? You think you change your hair all, can fool us meh?"

"Datuk Ong." Vellu put on a big, exaggerated smile. "How nice to see you again. How have you been?"

"Shut up lah," Datuk Ong snapped, and his gang members started to laugh. "Where the hell is my money? Interest damn high already, you know!"

"I'll pay you soon," Vellu pleaded. He fell to his knees. "I just need a little more time. If I win a few more matches—"

"Cannot wait! No patience liao." Datuk Ong rolled his eyes. "Want me to wait how long? Until I got grandson is it?" He cracked his knuckles theatrically. "My six hundred thousand ringgit! Now!"

"Last month it was two hundred thousand!" Vellu cried.

"Yes, that was last month! Who asked you not to pay?"

"Give me time," Vellu pleaded. "It's just—"

"Time's up!" Datuk Ong said.

He barked at his men in Cantonese. "Flying Daggers! Show him what we do to defaulters!"

"Yes, boss!" his men shouted. Then, as if on cue, they all withdrew small cylindrical toyol containers from their pockets. They flicked the tops open, in the same way one would flick a lighter.

Toyols emerged from each of them. These were smaller than the toyols at the pit, but just as deadly. They wore makeshift armor around their chests and arms. One toyol had a long metal spike attached to its headpiece, while another had a ridiculously long tongue, dripping with lime-green spit. The spit fizzled as it hit the ground.

Vellu screamed and ran, but the toyols pursued. They cackled and whooped and shrieked, their armor clinking loudly as they ran.

Two or three of them leapt, rising about four or five feet in the air before landing on Vellu's back. Vellu cried in agony and collapsed. The other toyols took this chance to pin him down, biting and slashing and tearing.

Around him the gang members laughed, Datuk Ong loudest of all.

Suddenly, a loud siren broke through their laughter. The gang members looked around in panic. "Police!" one of them screamed.

And sure enough, three squad cars were driving toward them. The gang panicked. They recalled their toyols and took to their heels. Datuk Ong panted and puffed as if he was having an asthma attack. He barely made it a few meters before collapsing, his hand on his heart.

Three uniformed police officers rushed onto the scene, led by Fara. She was smiling; it had turned out to be quite a fruitful night. Not only did they get a lead on the killer toyol case, but they had managed to take down the elusive Flying Dagger gang, who were responsible for many occult-related thefts and assaults in the area.

She walked over to the broken Vellu, who was lying in a pool of blood. He was missing several teeth, and his cheeks were covered with jagged scars. His clothing was torn, and he looked at her through bruised and bloodied eyes.

"Well, Mr. Vellu," Fara said. "I bet you're glad to see us now!"

# 17

## April 5, 11pm.
## Taman Asyik, Kuala Lumpur.

Another night out.

Ignatius's stomach was in knots as he added the last touches on his makeup. It was odd that he still felt this paralyzing humiliation, despite having done this almost a dozen times.

He took a deep breath. *This is a good thing,* Ignatius told himself. Made sure he didn't get too comfortable painting his face. After all, only women and fags used cosmetics. These negative emotions were a sharp reminder of how unnatural this was.

Anyway, this wasn't the sissy kind of makeup.

This was *warpaint.*

He looked into his bedroom mirror a final time. White face. Red stars around his eyes. Exaggerated red lips. It had literally been the first image to pop up after he typed 'clown' into Google Image.

*It's a good look,* he thought. *Friendly.*

Ignatius had always liked clowns. One of his few memories with his mother had been a trip to the Royal London Circus. He lived in Baltimore at the time. He had been impressed by the elephants and the tigers. But his favorite act had been the clowns. They were hilarious, with their custard pies and slapstick antics. They had made him laugh so hard that everyone in the audience turned to look at him. But he hadn't cared. He was having too much fun.

Most people didn't like clowns now. They were considered scary. They were the villains in horror movies.

Ignatius scowled. That was today's world for you. Corrupted to the core. Always taking what was innocent and cute, and twisting it into something perverted.

Well, thank goodness there were still people like him. Knights who stood for the old rules, defenders of good old-fashioned family values. Beacons of light in this corrupt world of sin. The world's only vanguard against debauchery until Jesus came back.

He put on his costume: a white shirt, and a bright pink jumpsuit. A bowler hat with a flower on it. Ignatius went to a cupboard and took out his equipment. An old-fashioned wind-up organ, which played "Old MacDonald".

The abominations were children at heart, Mr. Vellu had said. Nothing they liked better than a good ol' jaunty tune. There were runes on them that protected against magic, but music was fair game. They would flock to it like sharks to a blood trail. And the more organic the music was, the better. Nothing digital or recorded.

It also helped if you looked like a clown, or something friendly, the man had said. What child didn't love those?

Ignatius could not play any instruments, and so had bought this old organ off Amazon. It cost a fortune, but had been worth it. This old thing had netted him about seven of those abominations so far.

Tonight, he hoped to make it eight.

He snuck out of his house and hopped on his motorcycle. Ignatius thought of saying goodbye to his housemate Razif, but decided against it. The last time he had walked into his housemate's room, he had been doing awful, perverted things.

Everything that guy did was awful and perverted. Once, Razif had invited him to watch a video involving two girls and a cup. Ignatius had been expecting a nice movie about a tea party. Instead, he had seen horrible, horrible things, which had scarred his soul forever.

Ignatius sighed. Why had God tested him by putting him under the same roof as such a disgusting pervert? He prayed for Razif's soul.

It was quiet at the Taman Asyik Community Park. Very few people came here at night, and those who did certainly weren't good people.

It was the perfect place for him. The Lord worked in mysterious ways. It reminded Ignatius of how he would preach in Central Park with his uncle, many years ago. They would stand in the middle of a square and pass out Bibles, while Uncle Luke bellowed about how everyone had to repent now or face eternal damnation forever.

Not everyone had liked them. They had gotten into fights. Even been arrested a few times. But that was the price to pay, to be on the right side of the crusade.

Here, it was against the law to preach in public. Especially to Muslims. Ignatius truly missed America. That was Jesus Country. Where all the real action was.

Ignatius made his way to the middle of the park. Toward a shady grove, covered by angsana trees. A swing and slide set, rusty and dilapidated, unused for years. A row of dustbins filled with drug needles and empty beer bottles.

There was a small community center here. Originally, it had been used for community meetings and activities such as art classes. After the area had gotten a bigger, nicer center elsewhere, it had been abandoned.

And that made it perfect for him now.

There was someone standing at the entrance. Ignatius cursed.

It was a young woman, bone skinny, in a tiny denim skirt and a sleeveless black blouse. She was smoking a cigarette. She had almost as much makeup as he did.

She laughed when she saw him approach. "What the fuck? Halloween now is it?"

Ignatius said nothing. He would not respond to these sluts, lest he be tempted into sin.

"Excuse me," he said. "This is my place. I must ask you to leave."

The woman looked at him in disbelief. "This shithole is your house? For real?"

"Yes."

"What's that you're carrying?" The woman eyed what he brought with interest.

"My organ," he said.

"Wah, your organ is damn big!" the woman laughed.

Ignatius said nothing.

"Whatever," the woman shrugged. "Eh, want suck? Only fifty ringgit."

"Get away from me, harlot!" Ignatius snapped. "I need to use this place!"

"Aiyo," the woman cursed. "You want this place so much, you take lah." She was starting to get creeped out by this clown who spoke like a Biblical figure.

Ignatius was relieved the woman left. He entered the old community center, closing its broken doors behind him. He walked down a small hallway with doors on each side.

There were many rooms here, but he only used two. The first was to store weapons he had procured from Razif's cousin. This was the bulk of his arsenal, although he also had a few at an old locker in his uncle's old house in Kota Kemuning.

Razif had been insistent on not keeping guns at their house. "You bloody Americans and your hard-ons for guns," he sighed. "I know you can't live without them. But I don't want them to blow my face off, okay?"

Ignatius entered the second room: a large, empty space perfect for what he called 'the calling'.

The abominations were most active in the late night. They were strongest and fastest after midnight, and in the light of a full moon. That's what Mr. Vellu said.

It had been a true God-given miracle, finding him. Who would have thought that one of his hunts would lead him not just to a master of these toyols, but someone who worked for one of the largest toyol companies in the country?

Now, if only he could find the actual location of that company... Vellu had been frustratingly tight-lipped about that. What a pity.

But it was only a matter of time. One day he would get to the head of the snake. And then… there would be no mercy.

Ignatius crouched and drew a shape on the ground. Vellu taught him this weeks ago. A twisted curve resembling a cross between the letter 'D' and a Korean pictograph. Ignatius then took out a pocketknife, made a small cut on his hand and let his blood drip on the shape. It glowed red for a while, before fading away.

Now he was ready.

Yes, it was a shame he had to learn this foul magic. Sorcery was an abomination—suffer not a witch to live, the Bible said. But it was all for the best. These creatures could not be hurt by his guns. And wasn't it a wonderful thing, having the tools of the enemy turned upon themselves?

Ignatius took up his organ and started to crank its handle. He was sick of its melody by now, but had to put up with it. He hoped a toyol would show itself soon. He didn't want to be turning this organ the whole night. He would get the worst cramps in his wrist tomorrow. And that idiot Razif would make the most idiotic jokes.

Soon, the rune on the ground would vibrate. A sign that a toyol was nearby. It would be lured here, and Ignatius could cast his magic on it. Send it back to its master. Enact deadly vengeance.

Ignatius scowled. He hated all of them. These wretched perversions of life. The sickening masters who wielded them. The whores that spawned them. And most of all, the damned companies that mass-produced them.

It felt good, doing this. Abortion clinic protests, while fun, had started to feel like a lost cause. No one seemed to take him seriously, and Ignatius sometimes felt their protests were indirectly causing people to feel sympathetic for the other side. He didn't dare tell this to his uncle, though. He would have flayed Ignatius alive, for daring to suggest there was anything flawed with doing the Lord's work.

Doing this, on the other hand, actually got direct results. The mainstream newspapers barely covered his deeds. Online, however, it was a different story. The *Mysteri* magazine website published a long article about victims in Kuala Lumpur found drained of all their blood, by a perpetrator they called 'The Vampire Killer'. Ironic that for a publication that wrote so much about toyols, they didn't guess it was these creatures behind it. Ignatius had read that article with pride.

Killing perverters of human life with their own tools, making sure they would never be able to continue their dark deeds. It was only fitting. Surely he would get a place in Heaven. Ignatius's only regret was he could not watch the looks of horror on the faces of these scumbags as their creatures turned on them.

One day, Ignatius swore, he would destroy them all.

# 18

## April 6, 10am.
## Ismail's house, Kampung Attap.

Ismail opened his eyes as bright sunlight streamed right onto his face.

He rose from his bed violently. For a moment, he was seized by panic. *Celaka! What time is it now? I'm late!*

And then he calmed down. It was Saturday. No work today.

But why did the day matter? He never had to work a day in his life again!

Ismail yawned and scratched his stomach, before pulling his blankets up. He made a mental note to buy mosquito coils on his next trip to the pasar malam.

Wait. Shit, that was so like him. Still thinking like a poor man! No wonder he never went far in life. He was way, way above pasar malams now. He could now buy groceries at the mall. Or even at one of those atas supermarkets, the ones that called themselves 'Grocers'.

Not just mosquito coils for him, no sir. No, he could get one of those electrical anti-mosquito things, the ones that emitted high frequencies to kill pests. Ismail wondered how safe those were. He didn't want to go around the house with a high pitch constantly ringing in his ears. He already had Putri's nagging for that.

*Damn it. I'm still thinking too small.* He could hire a pest control agency to spray his house. He could buy one of those four-poster beds with mosquito netting around them. Shit, he could even hire a man to sit at his bed with a fly swatter if he wanted to. He was rich now, damn it!

And it was all thanks to his toyol. The best investment of his life.

Putri was still out, to her new gym in Bangsar Village. Ever since they had come into wealth, she had signed up for every fitness class known to man. Aerial yoga and Crossfit and Muay Thai and pole dancing and synchronized swimming and capoeira. He wondered how she had the time and energy.

What was for lunch? He took out his phone and selected the FoodSend app. Normally he avoided this, they charged exorbitant delivery fees. Now, what was a few extra ringgit to him?

He ordered Thai food. Ismail almost turned off the app, before making another order from La Risoto, and ending it with another order from a boba tea shop. Dessert!

He rubbed his tummy, which peeked out at him from the bottom of his singlet. *It must be shrinking in the wash.* This wouldn't happen if he had luxury detergent. He heard there were some that would make his clothes smell like strawberries.

Better yet, maybe it was time to get some new clothes. Where did one find a good tailor? Ismail took out his phone and called Harun.

No answer. Ismail turned it off and cursed. Harun had not been answering any calls or WhatsApp messages lately. Weird.

*Just goes to show that wealth really changes a person.* Rest assured, that would never happen to him. He would stay humble always.

He took a shower, using his brand-new shampoo (made from Korean honeycomb and sea anemone) and Tibetan body wash. He put on a pair of furry slippers and a gold-trimmed bathrobe, and walked downstairs to the hall. Ismail made a mental note to look into building a lift; stairs were sooooo lower-middle class.

Just then, he felt some vibrations in the pocket of his dressing gown. *Oh, thank God. Harun was finally calling back.*

He frowned to see the words 'UNKNOWN NUMBER' on its screen. This was true in one sense: this number had not been saved on his phone. But it had called Ismail so many times that he knew it well.

For a moment, he contemplated hanging up. Or throwing the phone out the window. He had always wanted to do that.

Instead, he picked it up. "Celaka!" he shouted. "Stop calling me!"

"Please, sir." A female voice. Muruku or whatever her name was. The friend of the pregnant girl they had gotten their toyol from. "We just want to see the toyol one time. My friend is—"

"I told you one thousand times. The answer is no!!" Ismail screamed into the phone, before hanging up.

Those stupid girls. Endlessly pestering and poking him!

Ismail had paid good money for the toyol. It was a fair transaction! When you bought something from a seller, did the seller have the right to go back and check on their goods every week? Hell no! The toyol belonged to him. A sale had been made, and they went their separate ways. End of story.

Ismail knew what they were planning. Be all chummy-chummy with him, become best friends, saying he owed them because it was her fetus and so on. Later, they would demand a cut of the toyol's thefts. And from there, move on to taking the whole pie. Threaten to expose him to the police if their demands weren't met.

Ismail knew. It was exactly what he would do if their positions were reversed. Well, fat chance. He wasn't sharing.

He went to the kitchen, looking for a snack. No more Super Ring for him! Now, he could buy potato chips in exotic flavors. Not just Original or Cheese or Chili—those were for peasants! He could snack on sophisticated variants like Wild Spice or Honey Mustard or Thai Tomyam. In fact, he could afford the very definition of decadence: potato chips that came in *tins* instead of packets! And pair them… with dips!

Ismail walked back to the hall with his snacks. He sat down on his new massage chair, and turned on his TV.

They made a lot of purchases over the last few days; best to strike when the iron was hot, Putri said. And this was his favorite one: Netflix. He had no idea he had been missing so many awesome TV programs!

He turned on his favorite drama, *Crash Landing on You*. Tragedy! Would poor Yoon Se-Ri ever get home?

Ismail took out his phone and took a selfie. *Life is good.*

Suddenly, his phone vibrated with a WhatsApp message.

From Toyols 'R' Us! So weird. He had never saved their number. The message read:

> Dear Sir/Madam, Due to circumstances beyond our control, we would like to advise you not to use your 'item' for the next few nights. You are recommended to—

Ismail was too lazy to read the rest. It was all bullshit. Not use his toyol? Ha! Were they stupid? Why the hell wouldn't he use his source of wealth?

He was rich! Rules clearly did not apply to him.

# 19

## April 6, 2pm.
## Toyols 'R' Us.

Lewis sighed.

"Look," he said, exasperated. "I told you once, and I'll tell you again. You signed a contract. Your toyol is now the property of the person who paid for it. And we can't force him to give you visits!"

"But surely there is something you can do!" Munira pleaded. Beside her, Jing stood quiet and demure, hands in her pockets. "I mean, the toyol was made from my friend's—"

"NO!" Lewis exploded. His face was a deep shade of purple. "I don't care if it was made from the blood of Buddha! There is nothing I can do. Now get out of my office before I call security!"

"Well, screw that guy," Munira muttered as she and Jing stepped out of Lewis's office. "I hope his balls fall off."

"Now what do we do?" Jing said.

"Try calling Ismail again. Give it one last shot."

"There's no use lah," Jing took a deep breath. "He's never going to give in."

They headed to the lifts and waited. One of the lifts beside them opened, and a pretty girl in a white uniform stepped out.

There was a toyol on her shoulder. Munira recognized her as Dawn, the Customer Satisfaction officer from their first visit.

Dawn appeared to recognize them too. "Oh, hello! You're… Jing, right? And Munira?" On her shoulder, her toyol raised its little hand and waved.

"Yes!" Munira said. "Nice to see you again!"

Jing cleared her throat. "Hey, you're a Customer Satisfaction Officer, right?"

Dawn nodded. "Yep. Why?"

"Well, we would like to make a complaint," Munira said. "We are not satisfied with your service."

"Wow," Dawn said, after Munira filled her in. "Damn, that's quite a story."

Dawn had taken them down several floors, to one of Toyols 'R' Us's conference rooms. These were brightly lit enclosed cubicles, each comprising only a desk and several chairs.

"So you want to see your toyol again, but the owners won't let you," Dawn said. She held a clipboard and pen, which she couldn't resist chewing on. Jungkook was back in his canister, on the floor next to her chair. "That is a tough situation."

"We appreciate anything you can do," Munira said with a big smile.

Jing was silent.

"I suppose I could write up a Visitation Order," Dawn said. "We have done it before. But it would take a long time… and Lewis would need to sign it anyway. And I think you've seen, he's not in a very good mood."

"Any reason?" Munira asked.

"Don't know if you heard," Dawn said. "But some of his toyols have been involved in crimes. Nothing to do with him or the company, but the PR has been really bad. A few investors are really worried, and the police are involved. So he's really stressed."

"We were surprised," Munira said. "He was very friendly when we first met him. Today, he seemed a real jerk."

"When Lewis is in a good mood, all is wonderful," Dawn said. "When he's not… ooh boy." She sighed. "He screamed at me for almost an hour yesterday. I sent out a message to all our customers. Telling them not to use their toyols for a while, due to this matter. And Lewis was furious. Said it was alarmist, raising a lot of fear for no reason. And it would affect our stock prices!"

She immediately turned back to them, penitent.

"I'm sorry, I really shouldn't be telling you all this! Please don't report me."

"No," Jing said softly. "Don't worry, we won't."

Dawn looked a lot more relieved. "Thanks. Sorry. It's just… it's been really stressful."

"If it helps, I think you're doing a great job," Munira said. "You were really helpful when we visited."

"Thanks," Dawn smiled.

"How long have you been working here, anyway?" Munira asked.

"About seven years," Dawn said, and laughed. "You know I started off as a client, not an employee?"

"What do you mean?"

"I first came to Toyols 'R' Us because I was pregnant. Just like you, in a way," Dawn sighed, and her pretty face grew downcast. "I was raped."

"Oh my god," Munira said. "I am so sorry."

"The guy got arrested," Dawn said. "But they let him go, due to lack of evidence. It was horrible. One of the worst times of my life. And to make matters worse, I was pregnant with his kid. I was young then, only 16, and I was terrified. I knew I couldn't keep the baby, but didn't know what to do with it. I didn't know anything about abortions, and even if I did, I couldn't afford one. And that's when I was introduced to Lewis."

She sighed at the memory.

"He was so kind to me. Unlike everyone else. He took me in, and helped me make Jungkook."

"So that's why you're working here," Jing said softly.

Dawn nodded. "Yeah. I needed some money after that, and nowhere else was hiring. And the company was looking for people, so I took it up. I wanted to help other young women like me."

She smiled wistfully.

"I really thought my life was ruined by my sudden pregnancy. I wanted to show other women in the same position that no, this wasn't the case. You have options. There is always hope."

"Toyols 'R' Us is really lucky to have you," Jing said.

"Thanks," Dawn said. "But the truth is, I've been thinking of leaving the company."

"Why?" Munira asked.

Dawn paused for a moment, before speaking again. "Me and Lewis… we don't see eye to eye on a few things."

"Like what?"

"Have you ever wondered… for the toyols that aren't created from supplied fetuses, like yours… where Lewis gets them from?"

"I thought they were supplied by volunteers," Munira said. "Or created in your labs."

"He does have people on his team whose sole job is to make him fetuses. Yes, they have sex with clients," Dawn clarified, seeing Jing and Munira's shocked faces. "And their goal is to get pregnant to make toyols. Lewis calls them 'brood mothers'. He keeps badgering me to be one of these. Says that looks like mine should create very beautiful toyols, which clients will pay top dollar for. But I don't want to do that, even though the money's good. To create a fetus, and then immediately destroy it, repeatedly... I think that's pushing things. I only created Jungkook because I had no other way, and the toyol procedure devastated me for weeks. I don't want to go through that over and over again."

"Oh yeah." Jing nodded. She too had been having nightmares... of being back in that room, on that horrible chair.

"That's not the worst of it. Brood mother fetuses make up only about 30% of his toyols. For the rest, Lewis's team goes to hospitals and refuge centers in small towns. They find young, single, expecting women, and persuade them to hand over their fetuses. Sometimes they're paid less than RM50," Dawn said.

Jing gasped. "Are you fucking kidding me?" Munira asked, her fists clenched in rage.

"He exploits these girls. He tells them he cares about them, he's trying to help them, but that's all a load of crap. Lewis doesn't care about anything except money," Dawn said. "He takes their fetuses, makes toyols, and sells them at a ridiculously inflated price. And he never gets back to them again. And the worst thing is, a lot of them take his offers. Most of them are scared, alone, disowned by their families. They don't know what to do and just want the problem to go away."

"There's a lot of stigma against unwed mothers," Jing said.

"But when we want to teach ways to avoid teen pregnancy, everyone opposes it!" Munira said. "It's stupid."

"Young mothers should be supported and helped, not judged," Dawn said. "Yeah, I was happy for Jungkook, in the end. But a lot of girls don't like that their fetus is turned into a creature that steals things. To be honest, I hate it too. To think we are indirectly responsible for crimes...But what else can I do? Honestly, once I find a new job, I'm so out of here."

"Good on you," Munira said. "Shit. If I had known how this whole place worked, I wouldn't have gotten involved at all."

"What will you do when you leave?" Jing pressed on. "Any way we can help?"

Dawn smiled. "I think I'll be fine. I'm taking a Business Degree over in Weaver's College now. Once I complete that, I'm applying for a new job." She took out a card from her bag and passed it to Munira. "I'm also helping out a local women's rights campaign. The Empowered Woman's Initiative. Heard of it?"

"Oh yeah! The one by Aini Hazliza right? She does good stuff," Munira said. "I'm glad you're part of it."

"Yeah," Dawn said. "It's badly underfunded now. But I have high hopes for it. She wants to increase sexual and reproductive rights awareness in this country. It's a long road, a lot of people have really outdated views here. But I think it's the only way to go."

"Keep up the good fight," Munira said.

"Thanks," Dawn said. "And I hope you get to see your toyol again. I'll talk to Lewis... but don't keep your hopes up."

Jing said nothing. She stepped forward, and gave Dawn a hug.

# 20

April 8, 3pm.
Brickfields Police Headquarters.

"I told you. It was for the bloody money," Vellu spat.

The Brickfields IPD interrogation room. Vellu, in an orange prison jumpsuit, sat at a table opposite Khairul and Fara. He looked awful, especially under the room's harsh fluorescent lights. His left eye was puffy and swollen, and he stank of sweat and piss. His hair was a tangled mess; birds would have loved to nest in it.

"How much did he pay you?" Khairul asked.

"More than you'll ever make," the prisoner sneered.

Khairul sighed. "No wonder we're known for taking bribes."

This was not a very pleasant morning.

It started off with the usual morning briefing. Khairul had to update their superintendent on how his investigation had been going on. And it had not been fun.

The moment Khairul mentioned the word 'toyol', the Superintendent choked on his teh tarik.

"Toyol?" he bellowed. Superintendent Leman was a large, dark man with a walrus mustache. "Is this one of your jokes, Inspector? Do I look like I'm laughing? DO I? Kau ingat ini apa? *Misteri Nusantara*?!" he almost screamed.

"No leads, no suspects, no evidence! What have you been doing all this time? And don't give me that toyol nonsense. Buang masa saja! The press is already breathing down my neck. The next time I see you, you better give me a solid lead! We cannot have another Gemas case on our hands!"

After that, it was time to catch up with Jairuz, with other case updates.

"Two more murders," Jairuz said. "Harun bin Bakhtiar, 36, and Wong Dee Shan, 71. Both in the Taman Perdana area. What should we do next?"

"Go to all previous murder locations," Khairul said. "And look for the canisters like you found last time."

"Those things? Eeeeeh. Geli!" Jairuz shuddered. "What the hell are they anyway? And why are you so sure you'll find them?"

"I'll explain once you find them," Khairul said. "Just find them quick!"

Jairuz left shortly after that.

After that, a positive development. Hafiz from Toyols 'R' Us sent him an email. Yes, he confirmed: all the victims, even the most recent ones, were clients of Toyols 'R' Us. All bought a toyol within the last year.

It was clear that toyols were indeed behind these serial murders. Now, they had to stop whoever was manipulating them, before there was another death.

Time was running out. Khairul was starting to get worried.

It was time for witness questioning. Thankfully, the Superintendent had to leave for another matter, and Khairul managed to sneak Fara into the interrogation room. Non-officers normally weren't allowed inside.

Vellu was not the most helpful witness. Every answer contained at least one swear word in one of several languages. Khairul was almost impressed. When it came to talking about his previous place of employment, however, he was more forthcoming.

Because he loathed Toyols 'R' Us.

Vellu had once been the local bomoh in Banting. Family business. It was a simple but comfy job, selling love spells and creating toyols for brainless villagers. There was constant demand.

And then stupid Toyols 'R' Us opened a branch in his town. How could he compete with them? They created toyols of high quality at ridiculous prices, with promotions and free umbrellas to boot! All his old customers slowly abandoned him, and he closed his practice within a month. How could a mom-and-pop shop like his fight against Big Toyol?

Vellu tried to get a job somewhere else, but failed. He had a gambling habit, and had done some pretty seedy things to get out of debt. He had gone to jail more times in his life than most people went to the dentist.

Eventually, out of desperation, he turned to Toyols 'R' Us. They were one of the most indiscriminate employers. In fact, many of their staff were drug addicts and vagrants picked off the street.

"And if you think that's because Lewis is some kind of fucking saint, you better forget it," Vellu snapped. "Thodiya pulle! He wanted people who would work as cheap as possible, with no other options. You think we want to work at a fucking job with dead babies all the time?"

Fara jotted all this down; that company was going to get a long visit after this was done, that was for sure.

Vellu was taken on as a toyol specialist. His job was to cast the spells and runes on a toyol before it was sent to a customer.

Two years on the job went by with little incident. He even got promoted to Toyol Delivery Specialist! He never thought he would be helping to deliver babies, but yet, there he was. The money was decent, and the hours weren't bad. Only problem was, Vellu hated Lewis with a burning passion. "Stuck up little asshole, prancing around like his farts don't stink," Vellu said.

The best part of the job had been the discovery of the toyol pits. Vellu was invited one day by a client, and fell in love with them. Especially since he worked in a company where he could bioengineer the best-quality toyols.

Vellu started participating, and did well. Thanks to Toyols 'R' Us, he created the biggest, baddest toyols, and dominated the fighting pits. 'Hurricane Vellu', that's what they called him. He made a small fortune.

But alas, all good things had to come to an end. His supervisor discovered he was using company property in the fighting pits, threw a fit, and banned him from them.

"Fucking punde," Vellu seethed. "Sitting on a fucking goldmine and didn't even know it! Fights, man, that's where the money is. Not selling to fucking Datuks and tai-tais. You only earn once. Fights, you earn every night!"

Vellu managed to smuggle away a few prize toyols, and did okay for a while. But things moved fast in the fighting pits. You had the hungriest and most talented bomohs and shamans, all eager to get their toyols as lethal as possible. Every week, the toyols got bigger and fiercer. One week, acid claws were all the rage, the next week all the toyols were sporting acid-proof skin. You had to keep evolving your toyols or you would lose out.

And lose out, Vellu did. Big time. His toyols kept getting beaten. But he kept on trying, hoping for a miracle.

The addiction cost him. He went broke. He sold his car. Took a loan from the Flying Dagger boys. But he kept on gambling, changing identities, locations, toyols and attack strategies. And things would have gotten worse—but then he met The Freak.

"It was, what, two months ago?" Vellu said. "I was in the Black Goat. The bar at the fighting pits. I was having a drink, when this weird bastard comes up. He struck me because of two things. One, he was a damn big guy. Like what, six-three? And built like a wrestler. But two, he dressed like a nerd. Plain white shirt, tucked into black pants. Like one of those fucking Mormons. Stood out like fuck. Too clean-cut."

Vellu rubbed his eyes, and coughed loudly.

"That pukimak chipet sohai. Got into an argument with the bartender. Wanted to see the manager and all that shit. Babi. Said we were all immoral and sinning against God and so on. Big mistake. They called security, and there was a bit of a fight. They threw him out."

"Then what happened?" Fara pressed.

"I kept on drinking," Vellu said. "Minding my own bloody business. Then later, I saw him again, as I was leaving the bar. He was lurking in the car park. I was a bit drunk, and needed a cigarette, so I went and talked to him. He wasn't very chatty at first. I teased him about how he got beaten up. And I ended up telling him I worked at a toyol mill."

"How did he take it?" Khairul asked.

"His eyes lit up! He seemed super interested. I thought he was one of those toyol stans, you know? Some women throw their panties whenever Hammerhead comes out. He asked me all sorts of things about the company, where it was, what it did, you know lah. But I didn't tell him anything. I still had friends in the company. I didn't want to send this monkey-molesting Bible loghiut to convert them all. But in the end, I told him how I cast runes on toyols. He was fucking interested. He asked me to teach him all I knew, and he would pay me."

Vellu cleared his throat.

"So yeah. I showed him everything. And he was true to his word. He paid me a shitload of cash. In US dollars! And that went well, until three weeks ago," he sighed again. "Who knew that Laughing Boy would slaughter Penyamun in a three-on-one cage fight? That fight was rigged lah. Stupid! Haramjadah sial butoh cibai cocksucking pundek sunni mayireh asshole--"

"Stop!" Fara said, and Vellu sneered.

"What's the matter? Too much for your delicate female ears?"

"No," Fara shook her head. "I need to write all that down. Some of your phrases are wonderful. I want to use them on some relatives."

"Whatever la," Vellu muttered under his breath. "Bitch."

"So you taught him about toyol runes," Fara ignored his remark "Including the bloodlust spell? Why the hell would you do that?"

"He said he wanted to learn everything," Vellu shrugged.

"Why do you even know that spell?" Khairul asked.

"I didn't. It was in my bloody company guidebook. It's impossible for me to know every damn rune by heart. So we made a copy." Vellu paused for a while, before gasping. "Shit, I shouldn't have done that, right?"

"Ding ding ding, give that man a prize," Khairul sighed. "Why did you answer all his questions? Couldn't you guess he was up to no good?"

"Well, yes," Vellu said. "But he was going to pay me big! And I figured the fucker couldn't do anything! No magic can work on our toyols! They all have anti-magic runes on them!"

"And you told him this too?" Fara said.

Vellu was silent for a while. And then, his face changed into a mask of horror.

"Yes," he said. "Lan jiao! I even told him the runes were on their hands!"

Vellu, unfortunately, could not remember the man's name. He did, however, have quite a clear recollection of his face.

"Big bushy eyebrows," he said. "But tiny little eyes. Tan skin. Very thin lips. Like a less handsome version of Ashton Kutcher."

Khairul ran a scan through an Identikit procedure, and did a cross-reference of criminals in that area. There were about a dozen results; one, however, stood out.

"Ignatius Hutch," Khairul read his name on the case file.

"Hutch?" Fara raised an eyebrow. "Orang mana ni?"

"Part Chinese, part American," Khairul read through the file. "A few prior arrests for mischief and assault. Spent a couple of months in Sungai Buloh."

He gasped. "Oh. This is interesting. It seems his uncle was the Reverend Hutch."

"Who's that?" Fara said.

"Some preacher. Led a megachurch in Puchong. Got in trouble for some fiery sermons he made years ago. Said that women were whores and they deserved to be raped and stuff like that. There were a dozen police reports made against him," Khairul said. "He used to live in the United States. Got arrested a few times for protesting outside abortion clinics. Threatened to blow them up. You know lah, fundamentalist stuff." Khairul smiled. "And look at that. It seems Ignatius got arrested a couple of times too. But he wasn't charged, on account of his youth."

"Let's look him up." Fara took out her phone. "Name like his isn't that common. Let's see what social media says."

She typed Ignatius's name into Google and frowned. Ignatius seemed to be a bit of a recluse. No social media to speak of, and only one really relevant link, to a PDF document.

"*The Incel's Manifesto*," Khairul said. "Written by our perp. Let's have a look."

"*How no one fucks you but the world*," Fara read the PDF's sub header.

"Well, we're off to a charming start. If you have any liquor, I would like a glass please," Khairul sighed.

The manifesto was about 100 pages, but felt much longer. Khairul had never read such an incomprehensible, whiny, repetitive piece of writing before. And he had once been the president of a Naruto fan fiction writing club.

The Manifesto was Ignatius's thoughts on the world today. According to him, men and women had very specified, defined roles in society. Men were supposed to be big and strong hunters and providers, while women were supposed to be gentle, submissive and weak. Men had to work and earn money, while women were to stay in the home and be docile while raising children.

"This would be regressive even for the 1920s." Fara had rolled her eyes.

Despite the manifesto starting this way, there was very little about men in the manifesto. Women, according to Ignatius, had lost their way, and were jezebels and harlots, going around acting in ways most unbiblical. This was backed up with what appeared to be a thousand Bible verses, all dripping with 'thou's' and 'yea's' and 'verily's'.

"All this talk about women," Khairul said. "Doesn't that make this a 'woman-ifesto'?

Fara groaned. "Reading this is painful enough without having your puns to deal with!"

This was followed by a long chapter on how the soul was sacred, and only God had the right to give and take life. Every tiny fetus was sacred and anyone who killed one had blood on their hands. Killing someone who slew the unborn was a just and valiant thing; better to kill one evil soul than let them take the lives of hundreds of potential lives. The usual fundamentalist pro-life spiel.

At one point, the Manifesto turned from sermon to journal, with Ignatius describing his experiences protesting outside abortion clinics. These were intricately detailed, with dates and event times included.

"'*These unholy places, these sights…*' I think he meant 'sites'… '*of mass murder! Slaughtering innocents by the millions! How dare they! I solemnly swear not to rest until I stop…*' Good God, this goes on for pages and pages," Fara sighed.

"I'll get some more coffee." Khairul shook his head.

Other parts seemed to be the ranting of a depressed virgin.

"*I am a man most virile in flowering, why has no woman looked fondly on me? Are they all harlots?*" it read.

"Maybe it's because you describe yourself as 'virile in flowering'?" Fara said.

The last part of the Manifesto, however, gave the most cause for alarm.

It started with a long poem, with terrible rhymes. How Ignatius was going on a journey across to the sea with his uncle, to Malaysia, the land of his birth. How his mission here may have been prematurely halted, but he looked forward to continue protesting at Malaysian abortion clinics.

"Hoo boy, is he in for a surprise," Khairul said.

The next few pages were that of jubilation. "*There are no abortion centers in Malaysia,*" he rejoiced. "*Even the most backwater shitholes can get some things right.*"

"Charming, isn't he?" Khairul said. "How did we not deport his ass back at the first opportunity?"

"Ignatius Hutch, Malaysia's Number One Christian Fundamentalist. I'm sure he was popular."

The next pages were that of listlessness. Life in Malaysia sucked, Ignatius wrote. He was bored and without purpose. He spent up to 14 hours a day in the States protesting at abortion clinics. Doing so had given him power and purpose. Without those here, what else did he have to do?

Things got worse after his uncle died. He had hanged himself in prison. Ignatius became tired and depressed, and thought about going back.

And then, the last page of the Manifesto:

*'Interesting news. It seems that although this country does not do abortions, it does something worse. Supernatural things, against the will of God!'*

*'It seems through the magic of the local witchdoctor, they can turn a lifeless fetus, most sacred of God, into something more evil, a beast they call a 'toyol'. This is an abomination and must be stopped!*

*There are even clinics where you can customize it to your own design and pattern. My heart trembles at the thought of such sin. Once I locate them I will cleanse them in fire. But they are hidden well like rats and will need to be smoked out.*

*'I swear that I will not rest until I wipe out the last of these foul 'toyols'. I make this solemn oath to the Lord.'*

# 21

## April 8, 5.30pm.
## Ismail's house, Kampung Attap.

"It's no use," Jing sighed. "They're not home."

"I know they are." Munira grit her teeth. "Look! You can see people moving!"

She pointed at what appeared to be a figure, visible through a small window.

"There! Right there! Answer lah, cibai!"

Jing and Munira were outside the gates of Ismail's house in Kampung Attap. It had a red, tilted roof and large windows, a small compound with an angsana tree and potted plants.

"Ring the doorbell again." Munira squeezed her arm.

"We tried seventy times!" Jing lamented. "They obviously don't want to talk to us!"

It was a hot day. Munira's black T-shirt was soaked in sweat, and Jing was perspiring heavily. *This was the wrong day to wear a long skirt,* Jing cursed.

They had been outside Ismail's house for half an hour. Jing had first tried to call them. All she wanted was to see the little toyol for one day a week. Was that too much to ask? But they refused. Soon, they even blocked her calls.

How could they be so cruel? Like it or not, she was the mother to the toyol, and had the right to see him.

Jing didn't understand why she was so attached to him. That toyol was, in all senses of the word, a monster. An undead, resurrected corpse, from a fetus she had never even wanted in the first place.

And yet... there was something special about him. A special bond had blossomed the first moment she laid eyes upon him. That bond had seared his image into her brain and heart like a fiery brand, and now, every moment they were apart made her depressed.

"Let's try one last time," Munira suggested. She started to bang on the gate. Munira had always been gutsy. To her, 'no' was only an invitation to try harder. It was how she had ended up the only woman in their college's previously all-male karate team.

"There's no point," Jing begged. "Let's go home."

Munira sighed. "All right. I don't think there's anything else we can do." She raised her voice to an unnaturally loud level. "Let's go home, Jing. They obviously aren't going to talk to us!"

"Really?" Jing said. "Are you serious?"

"Walk with me," Munira said, and drew Jing close. The warmth of her body next to hers was surprisingly pleasant. "Let's go."

They walked to the next street, before Munira stopped.

"Let's go get some dinner. Want to go to Sombreros? My treat," she said. "We'll need a lot of energy for what we're gonna do."

"Seriously?" Jing was aghast. "You can't be serious!"

"That's right," Munira grinned. "We'll come back later. And sneak in!"

X

At 11pm, the girls made their way back to Ismail's house. The street was dimly lit by a single lamp post. There were few cars on the road nearby.

"Time to climb," Munira said, as they approached the gates. Before Jing could say anything, Munira started to climb. In less than a minute, she had scaled over and was on the other side.

"Come on!" she hissed. "It's easy!"

"We can't do this!" Jing felt as though she was about to faint. "That's… illegal! We're trespassing!"

She had spent the whole of dinner trying to convince Munira this was an insane idea. But once that girl had an idea in her head, there was no stopping her.

"What else are we going to do?" Munira said. "It's the only way." She looked Jing straight in the eye. "Look. Let's find those two. We'll talk to them. That's all. And if they ask us to leave, we'll leave."

Munira held out her hand.

"Come on, Jing. We're going to see your baby again. Are you with me or not?"

Jing sighed. She had never been more terrified. Every cell in her body was screaming for her to go. She was never the kind to get into trouble; she had forgotten to hand up an assignment in secondary school once, and had sleepless nights for almost a week. To sneak into someone's house was something only criminals did.

And yet… why did it feel like the right thing to do?

Maybe it was the longing to see her baby again. Maybe it was for the guilt she would feel if she left her friend. And heck, maybe because there was so little excitement in her life as it was.

Jing said: "I'm with you."

"Excellent!" Munira beamed. "Come on. All you need to do is climb the gates."

"Easy for you to say!" Jing said. "I've never done this!"

"If I can do it, you also can," Munira laughed. "I used to do this often. I'd sneak out of school, like, once a week."

"No wonder I hardly saw you in class," Jing cursed as she took hold of the gates. "How the hell do you do this? It feels so... weird." She tried lifting a leg over the gate, but failed. "Damn it. I really shouldn't have worn this long skirt today!"

"Angle your foot!" Munira suggested.

"I can't!" Jing sighed. She tried again, but failed. Her long skirt made it hard to move.

"Damn," Jing said. "You'll have to go on without me."

"Don't be stupid," Munira said. "I'd never abandon you. Just a little— oh shit!"

There was a loud thud as Jing fell off the gate. Luckily, she seemed unhurt; she picked herself up quickly and dusted herself off.

"So graceful," Jing muttered. "Now what do we do?"

"Follow me," Munira said. "And keep really quiet."

The girls crept into Ismail's compound. They snuck around the angsana tree and went silently toward the house.

"Where are we going?" Jing whispered. "Isn't that the way to the front door?"

"Let's scout a little first," Munira said.

They circled the house quickly. Jing's heart was beating so hard she thought she might faint.

"There's a door there!" Jing pointed at one of the walls. It was red, with a silver handle.

"It's probably a shed or something." Munira shook her head. "What I'm looking for is a window. Here!" she said, pointing to one of the few windows that wasn't covered by a curtain or blind. "Let's have a look."

They peered into what appeared to be a cozy little store room. There was nothing in it except three large shelves leaning against the wall, each packed to the brim with bric-a-brac.

Munira struggled with the window and cursed. "Fuck, it's locked."

"Why the hell are we going in this way?" Jing was bewildered. "Seriously, why not just—oh."

Realization suddenly dawned.

"You're not planning to talk to them at all, are you?" Jing said, her voice cold.

"Ismail will never give us back our toyol. The only way is to steal it back," Munira said.

"Unbelievable! You want to make me a robber???"

"It is NOT robbery! It belongs to you!"

"No... it's... it... you know what I mean! I don't want to do this!"

"It's the only way!"

Suddenly, the door of the room opened. Jing almost screamed, but Munira covered her mouth and pulled her to the ground. The two crouched just beneath the windowsill, shaking with nervousness.

Ismail walked into the room. He was dressed in a batik shirt and sarong, as well as a cloth hat so garish you had to be extremely insane or extremely rich to be caught wearing it. Jing and Munira watched as he headed to one of the shelves, and moved a few items. He then withdrew a familiar-looking yellow canister.

"Jackpot!" Munira clenched her fist in triumph, while Jing hurriedly shushed her.

The girls kept peering through the window, not even daring to breathe. They watched as Ismail drew a circle on the floor, and then opened his canister. It took everything in Jing's soul to stop her from crying out as she saw her beloved baby emerge, a toothy grin on his face.

Ismail spoke to it; the girls could barely hear what he said. Then, suddenly, he stepped forward and hit the toyol on the head.

"Make sure you get better stuff this time!" Ismail yelled.

The toyol gave out a strangled cry; it was almost similar to the one uttered by Jing at this sight. Munira had to grab her, or Jing would have jumped through the window and given Ismail the thrashing of his life.

Ismail said a few more things to the toyol, before giving it his blessing. The toyol gave a high-pitched chirp, before bounding out a crack in another window. Munira and Jing could have sworn they saw a blur whizz past them.

Satisfied, Ismail walked out of the room, whistling a happy tune. The girls remained crouched for a few minutes, before Munira stood up.

"This is our chance. Let's go."

She tried to open the window again.

"All we need is to get in. We take the canister, and get the hell out. The toyol has to come back to it right?"

The girls did their best to force open the window, but it was bolted down tightly. Their combined efforts could not move it.

"Is there a branch around here or something?" Jing said. "Maybe we could use it as a lever."

"Wow, smart," Munira laughed. "You are a genius!"

Munira ran over to the angsana tree and broke off one of its low-hanging branches. There was a loud 'crack': Jing prayed Ismail and his wife did not hear.

The two tried their best to prop it under the window sill.

"It doesn't fit!" Jing cursed. "Maybe we need a thinner branch."

"Nonsense," Munira said. "It will fit, I know it!"

"That's what she said."

"You choose now to make jokes?" Munira rolled her eyes. "We're almost in! Just push a bit more—no, *don't push too hard*—"

But it was too late. Their efforts caused the branch to move violently. This caused it to dislodge one of the window panes, which fell on the floor, smashing into pieces.

The door to the room opened again, and this time it was Putri. She wore a dressing gown and slippers. She screamed to see the two girls at the window.

"SAYANG! It's them… the girls! From Toyols 'R' Us!"

"Fuck," Munira said. "Run!"

The girls raced toward the gate. Behind them, the front door opened and a red-faced Ismail emerged, wielding a broom.

"BERHENTI!" he screamed. "PENYAMUN!"

He lashed out with his broom, hitting Munira on the back; she gave a loud scream. She and Jing kept running to the gate.

"You go," Jing said, panting hard as she ran. "This skirt… can't climb gate… go!"

"No!" Munira said. "I'm not leaving you!"

Nothing more needed to be said. The girls abruptly changed direction: they ran toward Ismail, and then past him. Ismail was so taken aback that he stopped abruptly, almost tripping on his sarong. It would have been comical if things weren't so tense.

"This way!" Munira screamed.

As a last resort, they headed toward the red door they saw earlier. Munira flung it open and she and Jing raced in, panting. Once there, however, they realized they had made a crucial mistake.

"Shit," Jing cursed.

Munira's first guess had been right. It was a shed. Rakes, brooms and cangkuls leaned against a wall, next to paint cans, a stack of old newspapers and a wheelbarrow. There was no other way out.

The two girls turned, but it was too late. The red door closed on them with a slam, and there was a click as a key turned in a lock.

"Ha!" It was Ismail's rough, hoarse voice. He was panting heavily, but there was no mistaking the triumph in his voice. "Think you so smart, ah? You two can stay in there all night. I'm calling the police!"

Jing looked at Munira, trying not to cry. "Now what do we do?"

Munira embraced her friend tight. "Don't worry, we'll get out of here. I promise."

# 22

APRIL 8, 11.30PM.
TAMAN ASYIK, KUALA LUMPUR.

There was a group of youths hanging around a park. All male. Most were smoking.

One of them shouted as he saw the police cruiser approach. Everyone started to run, some of them tripping over themselves as they went in all directions. One guy even started climbing a nearby jungle gym. Did he really think he would escape?

"Weed smokers, probably," Khairul sighed. A very common experience on the job.

This was their lucky day, though. He and Fara had far more important things to do than go after juvenile delinquents.

They had been cruising all over Taman Asyik for over half an hour. Going past crowded mamaks and playgrounds and tiny little houses that all looked alike. What they were looking for, exactly, Khairul had no idea. But he prayed he would find it soon.

A referral to their police database had turned up Ignatius Hutch's last known address: a little apartment in KL. Jairuz was appointed to the case and after getting a warrant, he went there with a squad.

Nobody answered after many knocks. And so Jairuz and squad burst in. A loud yell rang out from one of the rooms, and Jairuz kicked down the door.

What he found completely surprised him.

There was a scrawny guy in the room. He wore only his boxers, and was lying atop what clearly looked like a plastic sex doll. There was a black wig on it, as well as very distinctive half-moon glasses. It looked a lot like local politician Aini Hazliza.

"I can explain!" the guy screamed.

Identification later revealed him to be one Razif bin Hadiman, 23. He was taken in for questioning. And boy did Jairuz have many questions for him.

Ignatius's room, on the other hand, was empty. Jairuz broke down the door to reveal a foul-smelling, dusty place hardly big enough for one person. Cockroaches skittered across the grimy floor. Bottles of expired milk sat next to old pizza boxes and styrofoam containers. Two bookshelves had Bibles and various religious books.

On a desk was a sketchpad full of strange abstract designs; a cross-referral with Vellu revealed they were toyol runes.

There were also several dozen boxes of ammunition, and a pistol in one of the cupboards. *Ignatius had access to firearms,* Khairul realized. *This is bad.*

A questioning of Razif revealed Ignatius had got them from him; he had a cousin in Thailand who could bring in firearms cheap. He supplied many of the gangs in the area. What worried Khairul was that according to Razif, Ignatius made several purchases over the past few months.

"I was going to tell the police," Razif said nervously. "It's just... it's just... I was busy."

So where was Ignatius now? Where were the guns? And what did he plan to do with them? Razif didn't know. According to him, Ignatius would go out by himself for long periods of time. He had no idea where he went.

A sweep of Ignatius's room with Fara's spellphone had better results. Hidden in one of his drawers was a folder containing his manifesto, Vellu's Toyols 'R' Us company manual, more toyol rune sketches, and a map of Kuala Lumpur and Selangor.

One site by Klang was marked on the map. Khairul recognized this as the location of the Pandamaran Fighting Pits. There was scrawled next to it in messy handwriting: *'Possible Thoyoll HQ? Must investigate.'*

There was one other site marked. It was in Taman Asyik, a housing area nearby.

There was a single word scrawled next to it:

*'Perfect!'*

And that was why he and Fara were driving all around Taman Asyik, their eyes peeled for anything suspicious. It only took about twenty minutes before they hit the jackpot.

"There!" Fara announced. "Look there!"

She pointed to a building not too far ahead. It was in the middle of a small neighborhood park, next to a dilapidated swing set and slide. Its walls were covered with ivy. A sign outside read, **TAMAN ASYIK COMMUNITY CENTER**. It looked, however, like the community had abandoned this place ages ago.

The windows were either broken or dusty. But there was light coming from one of them. Not any normal kind of light, but a strange, flickering orange glow. Almost like someone had lit a bonfire inside.

"Now that's suspicious," Khairul said. "Good eye!"

The two parked the car and made their way slowly to the building.

Khairul drew his pistol. "You armed?"

Fara nodded and pulled out what appeared to be a metal stick from her backpack.

"I thought you'd be packing a magic wand or something," Khairul smiled.

"You laugh," Fara said. "But this truncheon is runed. It breaks all magic it comes into contact with."

"Excellent," Khairul said. "Think we're going to need it."

The way into the old community center was through a broken door. Dead leaves were scattered all over the floor; Fara and Khairul instinctively tried to avoid stepping on them. Even one single 'crack' could give their position away.

"Hey," Fara whispered. "Do you hear music?"

Khairul nodded. *What the hell was going on?*

The duo stepped through a dusty hallway, with doors on each side. Only one door, however, had a clear bright light emanating from behind it. Khairul nodded at Fara; she drew her truncheon. He silently counted to three, before kicking the door down.

"POLIS!" he yelled as they stormed into the room. "JANGAN BERGERAK!"

What he saw shocked him.

A large man was standing in the middle of the room. He was dressed as a clown, complete with a white-painted face and red nose. He was cranking the handle of a large organ.

Three toyols stood all around a pentagram on the ground, with orange flames flickering in its middle. They were all dancing to the music. All were missing their right hands.

One toyol had a star-shaped mark on its head. Unlike the other two, his eyes were glowing red, and he was foaming at the mouth. "GO!" the clown, who was obviously Ignatius Hutch, screamed. The star-marked toyol leapt into the air, moving so fast that all they saw was a blur streaking past them.

The clown dropped his organ and pulled out a pistol. Fara and Khairul ducked as he fired a few shots. One shot flew just above Khairul's head; he silently thanked God he had not been two centimeters taller.

Khairul fired a few shots back, and it was the clown's turn to duck. He then shouted a few words in a foreign language. To Khairul's shock, the clown's eyes began to glow, and the tips of his fingers crackled with bright red energy bolts.

Suddenly there was a stabbing pain in his arm. Khairul screamed as he realized a toyol had leapt on him. It had moved so silently he wasn't able to sense it. He dropped his pistol in agony. Before it could hit the ground, it was snatched up by the same toyol, which leapt up and caught it in midair.

"Fuck!" Khairul screamed. He reached into his pocket to call for backup; he cursed again to find his phone missing. And so were his keys.

The second toyol struck when he was dealing with the first. It was bounding back to Ignatius now, who took the stuff it had stolen, a bemused look on his white-painted face. He then pointed at Fara.

The toyol screeched and leapt at her. Fara screamed, and lashed out with her truncheon. It was a terrific swing: the inspector had a promising career in softball. Her truncheon connected with the toyol with a sickening 'crack'.

The tiny creature flew into the air from the sudden impact; it was a toyol when it rose, but it landed as a still, soggy fetus. The magic that had animated it ended after contact with Fara's truncheon.

While this was happening, Ignatius was still firing his pistol. He didn't seem to be a crack shot: most of his shots landed in the walls, or shattered the already broken window panes. Soon, he was out of ammunition. Ignatius cursed, and muttered another foreign word. The flickering fire on the floor vanished, plunging the room into darkness. He ran out the room's other door.

"Stop!" Khairul yelled. Ignatius had locked the door behind him. Khairul kicked it down. As the door fell, he was met by another surprise: the first toyol from before, who leaped onto his face, screaming and yowling.

Fara swung her truncheon again, knocking the toyol off Khairul and turning it back into a fetus. The two officers ran out of the community center, only to see Ignatius, unmistakable in his clown getup, speeding away on a motorcycle.

"We can still get him!" Fara said. "Let's get to the car!"

"No point," Khairul sighed. "That fucking toyol. It stole my keys!!"

"Shit!" Fara swore. "We were so close!"

"Call for backup?"

"Nope. Bloody toyol took my phone!" Khairul raised his fists, and screamed into the night. He kicked a patch of grass so savagely he almost lost his balance. He then shouted a few more profanities, before sitting down on the curb, a look of abject dejection on his face.

"Are you okay?" Fara came up to him, concerned. This was the most upset she had ever seen the jovial Khairul.

"I'm just..pissed, that's all," Khairul said. "We were so close!" He clenched his fists. "And we let him escape! With my bloody things!"

"You did all you could," Fara said. "They're toyols, right? They're meant to steal things. No need to feel bad."

"We almost had him," Khairul said. "We could have ended this! What if he kills again? I can't take another death!"

"We'll get him." Fara sat next to Khairul. She put her hand on his shoulder. "Don't worry, okay? We know who he is and there's nowhere he can run. The next time, he's toast."

"I hope so." Khairul sighed. He stood up. "Come. Let's go. I'll call for another car."

"I'm sorry about just now, by the way," Khairul said. "I got carried away."

The two were sitting on the broken, but still usable, swing set by the abandoned community center. They were awaiting their ride, which would arrive in about half an hour.

"You have nothing to apologize for," Fara said. "In fact...I don't know how to put this…but I'm glad for it, you know? Before this, honestly, I wasn't completely sure if you were taking things seriously."

Khairul laughed. "Hey, I don't blame you. All the damn puns, right? Bloody hell. Yeah, I know they're not very professional, but on my job, you see a lot of messed up stuff. Either you laugh at absurdity, or you let it fuck you up."

"I do things a little differently," Fara said. "Whenever I see anything I can't handle...I force it out of my mind completely. Detach from reality. I tell myself, do your job, just get through this, don't let it affect you."

"Does it work?"

"I'm still alive, I guess?" Fara shrugged. "Still sane. Relatively."

"That's good."

"Yeah."

There was a brief silence, before Fara spoke again.

"We really should be worried about Ignatius."

"No shit."

"For someone who just learned magic, he was pretty good at spellcasting. You saw what he did? Making the toyols turn on us? That was a Hypnosis Charm," Fara said.

"Hypnosis Charm?"

"Yeah. Gets people in the vicinity to do whatever you want for a short period. You've heard of people being bewitched by bomohs to hand over their life savings, or let people into their houses? It's probably a Hypnosis Charm. It's a tough spell, takes a long time to learn. But I think it's easier to cast it on toyols."

"Shit," Khairul said. "How did he learn to do that?"

"Vellu's company manual, remember? Seeing how Toyols 'R' Us works, I wouldn't be surprised if it's full of unsavory business practices. Maybe that's how he gets girls to surrender their fetuses."

"True," Khairul said. "What should we do next?"

"Let's call Toyols 'R' Us," Fara said. "Check up on any toyol customers near this area. One toyol got away. I wonder who's the poor unlucky bastard it will go back to."

Khairul's hand moved instinctively to his pocket: he cursed as he remembered his phone was gone.

"You have to do it. I gotta get a new phone tomorrow." He shook his head. "All my contacts, and messages and playlists, all gone."

"Yeah," Fara said. "What a pity. I was so looking forward to 'Baby Shark' for the five hundredth time."

Khairul gasped. 'Holy shit! Did you just…make a joke?"

"No!" Fara said. "I was just being sarcastic. There's a difference!" But there were small traces of a smile on her face.

"Oh. My. God," Khairul said. "You know, in this entire time we've met, I have never seen you smile even once! If it takes my phone getting stolen for that, then I am glad!"

"Don't be ridiculous!"

"You can laugh at my puns, you know. I spend a lot of time thinking them up. They're high quality."

"I beg to differ."

"It's not like I just…phone them in!"

There was a brief pause. And then, Fara laughed.

It started off as a few giggles. Then, it developed into a full belly laugh. Eventually, Fara fell off the swings and landed in a crumpled heap on the ground, doubling up with loud guffaws. Tears ran down her cheeks.

"Ya Allah," she wailed. "Why did I get a partner like you?"

# 23

## April 9, 1am.
## Ismail's house, Kampung Attap.

"Any luck?" Jing asked. She was sitting on a pile of newspapers.

"Just a little more," Munira said. "This is tougher than I thought."

Munira had been trying to pick the lock for about an hour. She was currently fiddling away at it with a pen and one of Jing's hairpins, having previously tried a bent paperclip, her house keys and a broken twig.

Jing sighed. It was hot inside the shed, and it smelled funny. The only light came from a single bulb on the ceiling. She really did not want to spend the night here.

"Are you sure you know how to do this?" Jing asked.

"Positive," Munira said. "I watched a video on lock-picking once."

"Oh my god," Jing sighed. "We're going to be here all night!"

"Do not doubt my abilities, young padawan," Munira said, still focused. "I'll have you out of here faster than you can say— oh fuck!" She turned to Jing sheepishly, holding up a broken hairpin. "You got another?"

Jing wanted to cry. The longer she stayed in here, the longer she was away from her toyol, which was probably being mistreated.

"Hey." Munira sat beside her. "I'm really sorry, all right?"

"It's okay," Jing said. "You were just trying to help."

Munira smiled. "You're beautiful when you cry."

For a moment, both of them said nothing. And then Munira kissed her on the lips.

Jing blushed; Munira quickly turned away. "I'm sorry!" she said. "Shit, I didn't mean to make it weird! I just—"

"No, no need to apologize," Jing smiled. "It's okay."

"I've had a crush on you for the longest time," Munira said. "It's just… I never had the chance to really talk to you. And you were so sad that day, and I… oh shit…"

This was the shyest Jing had ever seen the brash, confident Munira. She wanted to burst out laughing. It was the most adorable thing she had ever seen.

"Look, I don't know if you feel the same way," Munira confessed. "If you don't want to talk to me again, I understand."

"Don't be stupid," Jing laughed. "Why the hell wouldn't I speak to you again?"

"Oh God!" Munira was visibly relieved. "Does that mean—"

"We'll talk about this later," Jing said. "Right now, let's get out of here."

She walked over to a nearby can of paint and took hold of its handle.

"Help me," she said to Munira.

"What?" Munira was stunned. "You can't be serious."

"Oh, I am," Jing said, gritting her teeth as she strained to lift it. "If we swing this hard enough, we might be able to knock the doors open."

"You can barely lift that!"

"That's why I need your help! Are you going to help me, or just sit there looking pretty?" Jing snapped.

"Yes, ma'am!" Munira leapt up hurriedly.

X

In the house, Ismail was lying on his sofa, a box of chips and a bottle of Mountain Dew on the coffee table before him. *Crash Landing On You* was playing on his big-screen TV.

His leg was on a footstool, and his wife was giving him a massage. Chasing after those two girls, Ismail said, had completely winded him out.

*Big macho man, runs a little bit and acts like he just climbed Kinabalu,* Putri sighed. He was so much fitter when they first started dating. But ah well. That was what marriage did to you.

"Maybe we should call those girls' parents," Ismail said.

Putri yawned. "Why can't we just go to the police?"

Ismail's eyes rolled, and he sighed deeply. "Don't forget, sayang, most of the stuff in our house is bought from stolen money!"

"They can't prove it," Putri said.

"Still. We should be careful. Don't give them any reason to suspect." Ismail took a mouthful of chips. "We're rich now, have to lie low. After they ask to explain how we can afford all this, then how?"

"True." Putri nodded. She massaged her husband's feet for a while, before speaking again. "You know, sayang, maybe we should just let those girls see the toyol again."

"Adoi," her husband sighed. He did not move his gaze from the television. "Why lah?"

"Stop them from always harassing us. And besides," Putri said sympathetically, "if I was a mother, I would feel sad about not seeing my child too."

"Haven't you been listening to me? We must lie low!" Ismail said. "What if those girls tell people about us? Or what if they want a cut of our money?" He scratched his chin. "Speaking of cut, we need to feed it soon."

Putri made a face. "Eleh," she groaned. "That one your job, right?"

"No, sayang," Ismail retorted. "I really don't want to."

"You know I'm scared of sharp objects!"

Just then, Ismail's phone started to ring.

"Is it them?" Putri asked. "Babi, are they calling from inside the shed?"

"No." Ismail shook his head. "It's… Pakcik Din."

Harun's father. But he was in England now! Why was he suddenly calling?

"What happened?" Putri demanded as Ismail hung up. His face was suddenly white.

"I don't believe it," he said blankly. His head started to swim. "Harun… dead."

Putri gave out a tortured scream. "What? But how?"

Ismail paused for a while, before finally answering, "They're not sure yet. Apparently it was blood loss. But there's also been a police report, they are still investigating."

Putri started to cry. "We were supposed to have brunch! In Melbourne!"

Ismail couldn't speak. He slumped onto his new couch and took a deep breath.

Apparently, Harun died alone in his apartment almost a week ago. His body was not discovered until two days ago. Everyone assumed he had gone to Australia. But poor Harun hadn't even turned up at KLIA.

A chill suddenly ran down Ismail's spine. Harun must have died the night they called him. They were probably the last ones who spoke to him.

Ismail blinked back tears. He would miss his cousin. True, they hadn't got along, but he was family. He wondered if Nenek already knew about this, and how she would react.

At least the last days of his life were nice. Harun had lived in luxury. But all that wealth, all those friends, and he still died alone at home. No amount of money could save you from death.

A dark thought entered his mind: *Did Harun's death have anything to do with his toyol?*

His thoughts were interrupted by a loud crash, which made Putri jump.

"What the hell?" Ismail leapt to his feet. "Is it the girls?"

"No," Putri said. "It came… from the guest room!"

The looked at each other in fear.

"Toyol!" they both screamed.

Ismail and Putri raced to their guest room, their hearts racing.

They beheld an ugly sight.

Their toyol had returned. But there was something different about him. Its eyes were now bright red, and it was foaming at the mouth. Its tiny body was covered in cuts. Shards of broken glass lay on the floor all around it.

Ismail groaned. This was the second window he had to get repaired tonight!

"Stupid toyol!" he yelled. He picked up the broom from the corridor, the one he had used to chase the girls. This stupid thing was going to get the walloping of its life!

He swung his broom at it. At any other time, the toyol would have taken the blow quietly. Instead, it leapt in the air, causing Ismail to miss and fall on the floor.

"Celaka!" Putri cursed. She shivered; there was something about the toyol's dark gaze that made her wary. "Sayang, maybe we should get out—"

She never got to finish her sentence. The toyol sprung onto her husband, digging its claws into Ismail's face.

Ismail gave a frenzied cry and staggered backward. Blood spurted everywhere as the toyol slashed savagely at his face. He dropped the broom and tried to pry the toyol off, but one of its claws had become embedded in his flesh.

He gave one last scream before the pain overcame him, and he passed out. The toyol began to drink his blood greedily, sucking it up like a huge mosquito.

Putri screamed. This was a big mistake. The toyol looked up from its feeding and grinned to see Putri. It leapt off Ismail and ran toward her. Putri tried to run, but the creature leapt again and landed on her back; it was surprisingly heavy for such a small creature.

It was not long before Putri too collapsed. She could do nothing but scream as the toyol sank its fangs into her, drinking deep.

The pain was excruciating. But it would not stop until she was drained dry.

X

"Was that a scream?" Jing asked.

She and Munira were in Ismail's backyard. They were planning to scale the gate again (long skirt be damned!) when they suddenly heard a strange sound.

"I think so," Munira said. "It sounded like Putri. That woman is loud!"

"What's going on?" Jing was curious.

"Don't know, don't care," Munira shrugged. "Come on. Let's get the hell out of here."

Just then, there was another strange sound: a loud crash, followed by another scream.

"I think we should go check it out," Jing said.

"Are you crazy? After how they treated us?" Munira was incredulous. "We need to leave pronto!"

But Jing was already walking toward the house. "Something could have happened to them," she said. "Something could have happened to my baby."

The front door was unlocked, and Jing and Munira made their way into the house.

"Ismail?" Jing called out. "Putri? Everything okay?"

"Shit, this is some creepy stuff," Munira muttered. She turned a corner into another room, and gasped.

Putri was lying on the floor, unconscious in a pool of blood. There was a small creature on top of her, hungrily lapping up blood from a jagged cut in her back. It had a star-shaped scar on his head.

It was Jing's toyol. Bintang.

Munira gasped as she took in the sight. Jing did her best not to throw up.

*What the hell? Toyols weren't murderers! All they did was steal!*

"What should we do now?" It was now Munira's turn to look helpless.

There was something wrong with the toyol. There was a strange red glow in his eyes, a ferocity to the way it carried itself. Both girls had only previously seen the toyol for a short while, but they could clearly recall how it moved. Friendly. Gentle. Almost cute. This time it was aggressive, jabbing his arm into Putri's stomach like it was stabbing her.

"What happened to its hand?" Jing gave a strangled cry.

The toyol did not notice them. It was still lapping up blood. Part of Jing wanted to run away and not look back. But another part of her knew it was the wrong thing to do.

"Bintang!" Jing shouted. "Bintang! Stop this! Now!"

The toyol turned to look at her. Recognition flickered in its eyes. But this was only for a second. Bintang's eyes glowed red, and it snarled loudly, before going back to feed.

"We need to get it off Putri," Munira said.

Jing nodded. The girls looked around the room, desperate for something they could use. Munira grabbed some books off a nearby shelf.

"Eh! Toyol!" she screamed. "Stop!"

She started throwing the books as fast as she could. Most missed, but some hit their mark. Bintang gave out a cry of anguish as a *Kamus Dewan* flew into its face.

"And that's the definition of badass!" Munira quipped.

"Okay, Munira, run!" Jing screamed. "The toyol is—"

Munira screamed. The toyol turned its attention to her. Before she could move, it had leapt, fangs and claws brandished.

"Get! The! Fuck! Off! Me!" Munira tried to beat the creature off her, but it was too powerful. Bintang sunk its teeth into her leg, tearing through her jeans. She screamed in agony; each of the toyol's fangs was like a tiny jagged blade.

Jing wanted to faint. This was a hideous nightmare.

She raced to her fallen friend. Without thinking, as if she was possessed, she grabbed the toyol. With unexpected strength, she pulled it off Munira, and then, inexplicably, held it close to her chest.

"Jing! What the fuck are you doing?" Munira screamed.

The toyol shrieked and sank its fangs into Jing's breast. Jing gave out a cry, but stopped herself immediately. Bintang struggled and thrashed, trying to escape this embrace. But Jing held on, hugging the creature tighter and tighter.

"Bintang," she said. Her voice was calm, but strong. "Stop. Stop! This isn't you. This isn't what you are."

The toyol shrieked and bit again, but Jing did not make a sound. She kept holding the toyol close. Bintang kept struggling, but its efforts were weaker now.

Jing was feeling faint. Blood was gushing from Bintang's bites and scratches, forming a pool on the floor.

"Stop it, Jing!" Munira cried. "It's killing you!"

"I'll be fine," Jing said. But that was a lie. She had never felt this tired in her life. Her knees buckled, and she fell to the floor. But she made sure to still keep the toyol in her arms.

"Bintang," she said. "My baby. This isn't you. Please. I love you."

In her arms, Bintang still thrashed. But was it her imagination… or were its movements less ferocious now?

Munira rushed to her friend and propped her against the wall. There was a small smile on Jing's face. Tears, however, ran down her cheeks.

"All this trouble," she said. "For this little monster."

"Don't talk! Just rest!" Munira tore a piece of Jing's long skirt, now rather frayed from all the action.

"Lucky I wore this today, right?"

"You need rest. Let me bandage you up."

"No," Jing shook her head. "My baby… he needs to feed."

At her breast, the toyol had almost stopped moving. Perhaps it was drained of energy. Now, it could only extend his single hand like a man groping in the dark, swatting at the empty air. Its eyes were no longer red. Instead, they were a deep shade of brown.

The same shade as Jing's, Munira realized. How had she not seen this? In fact, how had she not realized how closely the toyol resembled its mother?

This toyol was part of Jing. And it…no, he, was beautiful.

Bintang was now smiling. "Krrr krrr," he chirped. The tone was unmistakably friendly.

Munira patted the toyol on the head. "Be a good boy, okay? Behave."

"He's always a good boy," Jing smiled. "You didn't mean to hurt anybody. Right, Bintang?"

The toyol cooed. Jing closed her eyes, too drained to speak any more.

X

It was a strange sight awaiting Khairul and Fara as they made their way to the house of Ismail Baharuddin.

Originally, they had wanted to head to Sentul, to check out another Toyols 'R' Us customer. However, they received news from headquarters that a 999 call had been made from this address. The caller mentioned victims drained of blood; Khairul put two and two together. They hurriedly requested another police car and rushed here immediately.

Two girls were sitting on concrete slabs outside the house. One had her hand wrapped in a piece of cloth. The other was sleeping soundly on her friend's shoulder. She held a toyol in her arms. He cooed happily to see the officers.

"Took your time, didn't you?" the girl who was awake said. She had short hair, and was dressed in a black blouse and jeans. Her tone was more amused than malicious. "I called, like, ages ago."

"Sorry," Khairul said.

Introductions were made. The girl's name was Munira, and her sleeping friend was Jing. Jing was the mother of the toyol she was holding.

"You might want to call an ambulance," Munira said. "There are two people inside, badly injured. They were attacked by this creature here. You may not believe it, but this is a—"

"Toyol," Fara smiled. "Trust me, we know."

"Damn. You police are much more open-minded than I thought."

Fara nodded. "There've been a lot of these toyol attacks going on nowadays. Some bastard is casting spells on them, making them savage."

"Are you guys, like, Scully and Mulder?" Munira asked.

"Something like that," Fara said. "Now come on. We've got to go to the station. We need to take some statements."

"Do you need to call anyone?" Khairul said. "But sorry, you may have to use your own phone. Mine got stolen recently."

"No worries," Munira said. She nudged Jing gently. "Come on, babe. Let's go."

Jing yawned. Her eyes widened as she took in the police officers. "Hello there. Oh shit. We're not in trouble, are we?"

Fara laughed. "No."

"Is my toyol in trouble?"

"No. He was acting against his will," Fara said. "Still. I think you might want to go to Toyols 'R' Us tomorrow. That's where you got him, right? Get them to check him. Make sure all the dark magic is completely gone."

"Now let's go," Khairul said.

# 24

## April 9, 12pm.
## Brickfields Police Headquarters.

"Well, those girls were quite nice, weren't they?" Khairul said. He was fiddling with his new phone.

"The poor things," Fara said. "Going through such a traumatic experience."

It was the following day, and they were in Inspector Khairul's office. Ignatius Hutch's files were on the table before them, alongside a few maps and documents.

"Any further updates from your side?" Khairul asked. He leaned back in his chair, shaking his legs restlessly.

"Nothing so far," Fara said.

"Nothing from Immigration either," Khairul said. "He's bound to try going back to the States at some point."

"I guess so," Fara said. "How is the new phone going, anyway?"

"Okay, I guess," Khairul said. He did not look up from his phone screen. "I've got it mostly up and running, but I've got a problem getting all my apps back. This phone is not very user-friendly. Half the programs are in Chinese!"

"There's another briefing at 3pm. They managed to get the guy. Razif's cousin. The one who sold the guns to Ignatius."

A search of the old community center had revealed a room filled with firearms. Forensics were still at work, but it was almost certain Ignatius's fingerprints would be found on some of them. What they needed to do was cross-reference them against a purchase list obtained during the raid of Razif's cousin's house. They could not assume that the community center was Ignatius's only source of weapons, Khairul had emphasized.

Just then, his phone beeped, and Khairul made a triumphant exclamation. "Yes! My Routefinder is finally reinstalled!"

"Well done," Fara said.

He fiddled with his phone. "I'm on my old account again. But it's going weird. Something's wrong."

"Like what?"

"I just received a notification that I checked in to Jalan Tun H.S. Lee five minutes ago," Khairul said. His brow furrowed.

"It's the address of Toyols 'R' Us," Fara said.

Khairul gasped. "Ignatius. He was looking to find that place, wasn't he?"

"Yes," Fara said. "But he could never find the address."

"I saved it on my Routefinder app," Khairul said. "On my old phone. Which he now has."

Fara turned white. "You didn't have a passcode or something?"

"No, I never knew how to turn that on…"

"Fuck."

"FUCK IS RIGHT!!!"

Just then, Khairul's phone beeped again.

*ROUTEFINDER: You have just checked into Toyols 'R' Us.*

## Toyols 'R' Us, Kuala Lumpur.

Lewis shook his head. "Once again, we are extremely sorry about how all this has turned out."

"I'd say!" Munira exclaimed. "We almost died, thanks to your product!"

Munira and Jing were in Lewis's swanky office. The Toyols 'R' Us founder was in full damage control mode, sporting the most sympathetic expression he could muster.

"And we are very sorry for that," Lewis said, his voice like honey. "But we are not liable for what amounts to product sabotage by a third party. It was not our fault that some psycho decided to cast these spells on your toyol."

"Fault or not, you really should compensate us!"

"Nope. You signed a waiver. It's in your forms!"

"Seriously?" Munira's eyes flashed. "Don't make us sue your ass!"

"Please," Lewis laughed. "Good luck going up against our legal team. We have some of the best in the business." He smiled. "I do sympathize and would like to offer some compensation. Please take these coupons offering 20% off your next toyol purchase."

"COUPONS?" Munira rose, screaming. "I'll tell you where to cash your coupons, you bloody son of a—"

"Stop, Munira." Jing took her friend's hand and gently pulled her down to her seat. "It's okay. It's all good."

She turned to face Lewis.

"Look, it's fine if you can't give us compensation. It's all right. What I need to know is, is my toyol okay?"

Lewis smiled. "Ah, finally. Someone *civilized.* I like you very much," he remarked, shooting an icy glare at Munira.

Munira stuck her tongue out at him.

He picked up some documents on his desk. "Well, according to this, your little guy should be okay. There were some very powerful spells placed on him, but nothing our bomohs can't deal with. You should be able to pick him up from the toyol pods soon."

"Oh, thanks so much!" Jing smiled. "I'm so happy to hear that!"

"No worries. We do our best to satisfy all our customers," Lewis said. He leaned forward and smiled at Jing. "Hey, you know, you really are a beautiful girl. Would you be interested to join our company? A lot of people would pay big bucks to make a toyol with you."

"Thanks, Mr. Lewis," Jing said. "But no thanks."

"Go fuck yourself." Munira flashed him her middle finger. "Come on, Jing. Let's go."

Lewis, however, was not giving up. He threw them another sales pitch.

"Can I interest you in any other products? We have a sale of Thai—"

He was interrupted by a loud scream. This was followed by two deafeningly loud sounds.

"What the fuck?" Munira cursed.

"That sounded like—" Lewis said.

"Gunshots!" Jing said, in panic.

Lewis picked up the phone on his desk. "Hello? Security? Hello?" He slammed the phone down in fury. "No one's answering!"

Suddenly, the door swung open, and a girl burst through. It was Dawn, a look of absolute terror on her face. Jungkook was perched on her right shoulder, also looking concerned. Their resemblance was unmistakable.

"Dawn!" Lewis exclaimed. "What's going on?"

"Sir," the girl said, breathless. "Some psycho has come into the building. He's shooting everyone!"

"Call the police," Lewis said.

"We have! But what do we do till they get here?"

Lewis's face was deathly white, and his hands were trembling. "Oh my god. This is not happening."

There was another gunshot. Dawn cried out in fear. Munira hurriedly shushed her.

"We need to get out of here," Munira said. "Lewis. What's the best way out?"

"There's the front way," Lewis said. Gone was his confident swagger, his honeyed tones. "Where you came in."

"That's probably where the gunman came in. Anywhere else?"

"There is a back door. Where we pick up deliveries."

"Then that's our best chance. Lead us there, quick," Munira said. "And keep low."

Munira, Jing, Lewis, and Dawn slowly made their way through the building, crouching low on the floor. Dawn was crying silently, and Lewis was quivering like a leaf.

Normally, a place like this would be filled with the soundtrack of office life: telephones, photocopiers, people. Now, it was almost silent. The only sound was the Toyols 'R' Us theme song, which was still playing on the PA system.

*'Toyols 'R' Us!*
*Baby we're the best!*
*You can't beat us*
*So don't delete us*
*We've got the need-sus*
*Of your fetus*
*We're not kidding around!'*

The occasional sound of a gunshot rang through the air; everyone would flinch, and Dawn would weep. Jungkook would give out a pained cry, and his mother had to silence him.

"We need to get to the lift," Lewis said. "Then get to the ground floor, and make our way to the back."

"Too risky," Munira said. "What if the lift takes too long? Or we get trapped in there with him?"

"You want to climb down eight flights of stairs?"

"Do we have any other choice?"

"Let's just go," Jing said solemnly. "There's no time to argue."

Finally, the four reached the stairs. There was a dead man's body before them. His white shirt was covered in blood, and there was a nasty wound on his forehead.

"Hafiz!" Lewis gave a strangled cry. "No!"

Munira shushed him. "That will be us if we don't get out of here!"

Just then, there was the sound of footsteps, and a door opening behind them. Everyone froze in panic.

Ignatius walked into the Toyols 'R' Us office.

Getting here had been a pain. All the secret doors and codes and what the fuck. He managed to bypass all of them, however, by blasting his way through doors, or forcing other people to open paths for him. Nothing was more persuasive than the barrel of a shotgun.

There seemed to be no one here; part of him, he had to admit, was relieved. Killing people was more of a strain than he had expected.

His first kills were done almost on reflex. They were the first two employees who had approached him upon his entry. He shot and killed the first immediately; the second fell to her knees and begged for mercy. Ignatius responded by shooting her in the face.

He thought he would feel great about it. Here he was, purging the world of those who created the abominations. And yet, there was no feeling of triumph. Instead, he couldn't help but feel… horror.

He had actually taken a life. Two, in fact. There was blood on his hands. Yes, he had talked about killing, dreamed about doing so, but now that he had actually done it… it was different. Watching two people die in front of him… the agony on their faces would be something that would always haunt him.

*Those two people I killed, they probably had families, loved ones, and thanks to me, they would never see them again…*

For a moment, Ignatius felt like crying. He suddenly saw his actions in a grim new light. What was he doing? Defending the sanctity of life by… killing people? It made no sense.

But it was too late to stop. He started this mad plan, and now he had to see it through. If they caught him, they would throw him in prison. He suddenly remembered his uncle, who hanged himself in his cell…

Ignatius reminded himself of his mission. He was a crusader of God, here to uphold His word. He could not be swayed by emotion.

He would shoot five more people as he walked through the building. With every shot, he forcefully told himself: *This is for the greater good.*

The gunman was a tall, burly man, in a black T-shirt and army print trousers. There were bloodstains all over him, and he clutched a shotgun.

He scowled as he saw them. "Ah." His voice was deep, with the faint trace of an American accent. "More disciples of murder!"

He fired; all four were able to duck just in time. The bullets whizzed over their heads and into the wall of one of the cubicles behind.

"So many women," He shook his head. "I should have known this place would be full of them. Damned sluts."

He fired again, causing the four to scatter in all directions.

"Please!" This was Lewis, cowering in a corner. "Let me go! I'll pay you anything!"

"So you're the boss of this establishment," the gunman said. He walked toward him, holding his shotgun high. "Tell me. Where are all the toyols kept?"

He pronounced the word as 'thor-yols'; in any other circumstance, everyone might have laughed.

"They're all on the sixth floor. In the toyol pods," Lewis said. He was in tears. He pulled out a keycard from his pocket. "Here. Use this to enter. Just don't hurt me."

The toyol pods! Jing suddenly felt dizzy. Wasn't that where Bintang was?

The gunman snatched the keycard from Lewis and grinned. "Thank you. You've been so helpful. Now, get the hell out of here."

A grateful Lewis stood up and raced past them to the stairs. His pants were soaking wet.

The gunman started to walk around the office. "I dreamed of finding this den of sin for ages," he said. "So I'm going to take my damn time."

He fired his gun into the air; there was a scream. It was Dawn, on the other side of the office. The gunman smiled as he walked toward her.

"You should be ashamed of yourself," he called out. "Turning the unborn into these unholy abominations. Rot in hell!"

Dawn was trapped in between a row of cubicles; there was nowhere she could go without running into the gunman again. She kissed her toyol on the head.

"Go, Jungkook. You know what to do."

Her toyol nodded, then raced away on all fours.

Munira crept to see Jing, who was hiding behind a desk, trembling.

"We need to go now." Munira motioned to the lifts; there was a clear path to them, now that the gunman had moved toward Dawn. "It's our only chance."

To her surprise, the white-faced Jing shook her head. "We can't leave Dawn. And we can't leave my baby."

"Are you crazy? We can't stop him!" Munira wanted to scream. But the fire in Jing's eyes told her she would not change her mind.

"Your noble heart will be the death of us," Munira cursed.

At the opposite end of the room, the gunman approached Dawn. "Such a pretty face," he said solemnly. "But you HAD to participate in this slaughter."

He shot Dawn in the leg; she collapsed, screaming.

"As I said," the gunman said nonchalantly, "I'm going to take my time."

He raised his shotgun again. Before he could shoot, there was a scream from another direction. The gunman turned.

"Now!" Munira shouted. She and Jing both rushed at the gunman. They came at him from opposite directions; taken by surprise, he had no idea where to shoot.

Neither girl was what you would have called 'heavy'; combined, however, their collective body weight was enough to knock him to the ground. They attacked every way they could, kicking, biting and punching.

"Fucking sluts!" he screamed. He dropped his weapon and grabbed Jing, savagely tossing her off him. He kicked Munira into a corner.

"No!" Jing screamed.

The gunman picked up his shotgun. He aimed it at Munira.

"Fucking die!" he screamed and pulled the trigger.

Munira closed her eyes.

*Click click.*

A few meters away, Jungkook the toyol raced back to his mother, who was still lying in a pool of blood. The blood smelled wonderful; he wanted to lap it up. But he knew he couldn't. It was his master's blood, and he would not eat it without permission.

He held out his precious cargo to her with a grin.

Jungkook had not been strong enough to steal his target's weapons. But he had managed to steal its ammunition, and the bullets the man was carrying. He had taken his chance during the split second the gunman had dropped his weapon.

He smiled at his mother. Did he do a good job?

"You did wonderful." Dawn smiled weakly. She was about to faint.

Ignatius was baffled. *Fuck! Of all the times to run out of ammo!* And he could have sworn he had packed extra!

This was not looking good. In front of him, one of the girls who had knocked him down was getting on her feet. She had short hair, and wore a blue blouse and jeans.

*Well. Time to do this the old-fashioned way.*

He pulled out his knife from his belt. Ignatius raced to her and slashed; to his shock, Munira ducked and lashed out with her feet. He was knocked to the ground, yet again.

*Fuck! Not again! If Razif heard about this, he'd never let him live it down!*

Ignatius gave out a primal yell and grabbed Munira's arm. She put up a fight, twisting his arm into an excruciating painful angle. Ignatius felt like he was going to black out. But he couldn't. His pride wouldn't allow that.

He mustered his strength and threw the girl to the floor. He raised his blade and got ready to strike. Just then, there was a gunshot, and a bullet whizzed past his ear.

Ignatius screamed and turned.

"Put down your weapon!" Khairul yelled as he, Fara, and a team of policemen burst into the room. "Get on the ground!"

The gunman cursed. He turned to the girl he had almost stabbed and recited some foreign words. To everyone's horror, Munira picked up a nearby chair and walked toward the policemen. She started swinging it at them violently.

"Munira!" Jing cried. "What are you doing?"

"Bloody Hypnosis Charm!" Fara cursed. She ran forward and raised her truncheon. "Sorry for this!"

She tapped Munira on the head with it; the girl collapsed with a groan.

The gunman cursed. He took to his heels and ran out a nearby door.

"Celaka!" Khairul cursed. He directed the other officers to take care of the wounded girls, before turning to Fara.

"Come on!" he shouted. "He's not getting away again!"

The door led to a small corridor, which in turn led to a stairwell. The only way was down.

Ignatius was a distance away from them. Fara and Khairul followed in hot pursuit down the stairs.

Khairul fired a few shots; whether through reflexes or magic, Ignatius dodged them all. He had too much of a head start: two floors below them already, and covering a lot of ground.

"I'm running out of ammo," Khairul cursed. "And he's running out of this place!"

"Still you have time to pun," Fara sighed. "I'm going to try something."

She took out her truncheon. Fara craned her neck over the stairwell, looking for Ignatius. He was a few floors beneath her, still running fast.

Fara waited until he was just beneath her…

… and then dropped her truncheon.

The truncheon spun in the air as it fell, spinning and spinning…

…it landed directly on Ignatius as he ran, three floors below her, landing smack on his shoulder. He cursed in pain as he fell to his knees.

"Holy shit that was AMAZING!" Khairul exclaimed.

Her timing had been just perfect! But there was no time to cheer. Fara and Khairul raced down to where he was.

When they arrived, however, he was nowhere to be seen. The only thing left there was Fara's truncheon, lying lonely on the floor. Somehow, despite being subdued by the truncheon, that slime Ignatius Hutch had managed to make his escape again.

Both officers cursed.

The other police officers soon arrived; it was discovered that Ignatius had used Lewis's keycard to open a door on the bottom-most floor.

"That door," Fara asked Dawn. "Where does that lead to?"

"The spellcraft laboratories," Dawn said. "He can get to the front door from there."

Fara nodded. "I'll get a team. He is definitely not getting out of here."

As she made her way out, she passed by an injured Jing.

"You guys again," a bemused Jing said. "Would it kill you to arrive on time for once?"

"Search every hallway," Khairul said into his walkie-talkie. He was in the basement, outside the labs they had seen on their previous visit. "He has to be in the building somewhere!"

"Roger," Jairuz radioed back. "We have teams stationed at every exit."

Khairul shut off his walkie-talkie and frowned.

There were only two exits. Both had police teams lying in wait. But it had been half an hour already. Where the hell was he? He couldn't let this monster get away again!

Just then, a man walked up. It was Ah Chuan, the doorman of Toyols 'R' Us. He had suffered minor injuries from the attack, but survived by lying still and playing dead.

"Eh, Tuan," he said. "I think you should see this."

Ah Chuan led him into the spellcraft laboratories. It looked exactly the same as it did when Khairul and Fara had visited, except for one major difference.

The large steel cover in the middle of the room had been moved, revealing a gaping hole.

"Yes," Ah Chuan said. "He go in."

"Shit," Khairul said. "Where does that lead again?"

"Sewer," Ah Chuan said.

"I better call my team," Khairul said. He took out his walkie-talkie, but the doorman took his hand gently.

"No," he said. "You dowan go there. Trust me."

"What?" Khairul was stunned. "But why? Didn't you use it to— oh."

"Throw away failed experiment." Ah Chuan smiled. "Oh, yes. Last time have to clean there every month. But then, have to stop. Too dangerous." He pulled up his trousers to show his prosthetic leg. "How you think this happen?"

# 25

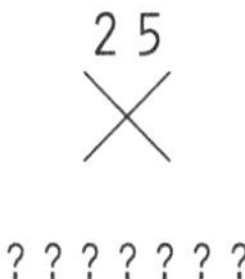

## ? ? ? ? ? ? ?

Ignatius cursed. The battery on his phone was dying; once that was gone, there went his only source of light. He waved his phone flashlight around: there was nothing ahead of him but darkness, darkness, and more darkness.

How long had he been wandering these sewers? He had no idea. That hole in the lab had led to a flight of stairs, which led to a network of tunnels, each leading into an intricate network of other tunnels. This fucking labyrinth seemed to go on and on and on.

He muttered another spell and snapped his fingers; to his shock, nothing happened. *What the hell? Wasn't this supposed to create a beam of light?*

Ignatius had no way of knowing this, but he now had no magical ability at all. That little encounter with Fara's anti-magic truncheon had seen to that. Until he recharged at a mana pool, he was now as magical as a magic marker.

Which was to say, not magical at all.

He had tried to use strategy. Only turning left whenever he had to make a choice. But that was dozens of tunnels ago. How far he had gone, and how deep he had ventured, he had no idea.

Ignatius had taken off his shirt and tied it around the lower half of his face; the smell here was hideous. Like something dead and rotten had taken a bath in the fluids of another dead and rotten thing. Ignatius had vomited when he first entered. All over his new Nikes too.

He could forget about his shoes, though. They were probably completely destroyed. The ground was covered with muck and dirty water. He squelched at every step.

Ignatius thought of calling Razif. But he had no reception down here and needed his battery for his flashlight. How could that idiot help him out, anyway? Wank all over him? That was all that perv knew how to do.

He kept walking. Ignatius groped in the dark, hoping to find some kind of ladder to the surface. He mouthed a desperate prayer.

*At least I'm away from the police*, he thought. Damn, he would not last long in prison.

Just like his uncle.

Ignatius suddenly felt a tinge of sorrow for his dead uncle. It was quickly replaced, however, with hate.

*This is all your fault*, he thought angrily. *If we had stayed in America, I would still be happily protesting outside abortion clinics. Not wading ankle deep in shit.*

It was just then that he heard a high-pitched chirp.

What? That sounded like… no, it couldn't be! What would a toyol be doing down here?

Ignatius aimed his flashlight at the source of the chirp.

What he saw chilled him to the bone.

It was, indeed, a toyol. But an ugly one, even by their standards. Its face had been split open, revealing a grubby, half-eaten brain.

Behind it, many other toyols were approaching. Most were crawling; some were skittering, insect-like, on the walls. Others were slithering on the ceiling, leaving glowing trails of slime. Some were wading through the water, and one or two were... flying?!

Hundreds of them. All hideous. Some had misshapen features, some were missing arms or legs, others had intestines or their brains showing. One toyol ran on a tiny body and legs, dragging a huge, balloon-like head behind it. Another was a mass of noses, attached to a slug-like body. There were two-headed toyols, three, some even with four. One toyol with three smaller heads bulging from its legs. One toyol that oozed blood out of hundreds of little holes in its skin. Toyols with arms or genitals where their heads should be. Toyols with massive fangs jutting out of their broken jaws and toyols with huge, staring eyes that took up their entire faces.

Ignatius screamed. He was out of ammo; besides, it would have been useless against these creatures. There was nothing he could do but turn and run.

The grim parade of misshapen toyols chirped and gibbered as they followed him. These sounds merged with a dozen others: the beating of broken wings, the splish-splosh of sewer water, the pitter-patter of thousands of little feet all moving at once. The toyols moved at a snail's pace, not bothering to hurry. They knew their prey would tire. It was only a matter of time.

Filled with panic, and in the low light, Ignatius did not notice a wall in front of him. He collided into it with great force and fell on his back with a splash.

A cacophony of cricket-like chirps rose up: the toyols were *laughing.*

Ignatius tried to stand up again. It was hard, with his head spinning from pain and panic. He put his hand against the moss-covered wall to sturdy himself.

A toyol came up to him. The one with the half-eaten brain. It chirped one word at him.

Despite living in Malaysia for five years now, Ignatius had not been able to pick up Malay. But he was very familiar with this particular word.

*Lapar.*

Hungry.

He pulled out his knife. Involuntarily, tears came to his eyes. This was not how he wanted to make his last stand, damn it. How the fuck had it come to this?

He was suddenly aware of a stabbing pain. The toyols were pouncing on him; one had sunk his teeth into his arm.

Ignatius screamed and slashed it with his knife. The toyol fell into the murky water with a splash.

The other toyols began to chirp loudly. As if they were cheering.

And then, in a great swarm, they all leapt on Ignatius at once.

Ignatius struck out with his knife, again and again, but there were too many of them. The toyols latched onto every part of his body, biting, slashing, ripping.

"Lord!" he cried. "Why hast Thou—"

They were the last words he ever said. For at that moment, a two-headed toyol latched onto his head, tearing off his tongue.

His eyes were the next to go. The only positive thing that can be said was that death came quick and certain. And poor Ignatius Hutch did not have to wait long until he blacked out, every drop of his blood lapped up by these forgotten toyols, some of which had not been fed in years…

# 26

## April 13, 2pm.
## Hospital Bangsar.

Ismail opened his eyes. His head felt like it was on fire.

Where the hell was he? Ismail took in his surroundings. He was lying in a bed. Bandages were wound tightly around his arms and chest, and there was a drip attached to him. Flowers and oranges were on a table next to him.

"Sayang dah bangun!"

His wife was sitting at the foot of his bed. She was in a blue baju kurung, and her hand was in a sling.

"How are you feeling?" Putri went up to him and held his hand gently.

"What happened?" he asked.

And then it all came back to him. The two girls. The toyol. How he was attacked.

Ismail struggled to get out of his bed, but his wife tried to calm him down. "Don't struggle!" she hissed. "It will make things worse!"

"Where is this?" he asked.

"Hospital Bangsar," Putri replied. "We were sent here after that toyol attack. You know we thought you were dead? You weren't breathing for so long!"

Ismail felt a throbbing pain in his head. The events of the previous days flashed in his mind; they seemed so surreal now.

"What did the doctor say?" he asked.

"You'll need to be here for a few days more. Observation. We both had major blood transfusions," Putri said.

"Transfusions?" Ismail now felt like his head was spinning.

"The doctor was very baffled. Never seen a case like this before, he said. But you were very lucky. Any later, you could have died of blood loss!"

"What happened to our toyol?"

"Oh," Putri said. "We had to give it back."

"Really?" Ismail almost yelled. "But why? That was our big ticket!"

"You gila ke?" Putri screamed. "After what it did to us?"

A nurse walked by. "Please lower your voices," she said. "This is a hospital!"

Putri hurriedly apologized, before turning back to Ismail. "Besides. Giving it back wasn't my idea. It was the police."

"The police?" Ismail actually felt his blood pressure rise. "They… didn't ask anything, did they?"

"No, not really," Putri said. "They were from some special branch of Bukit Aman. They asked us to hand over our toyol because it was needed as evidence in a case."

"Oh," Ismail said. "So I guess you had no choice."

Putri nodded. "I think it's for the better. I never want to see another toyol again! I knew it was a bad idea from the start."

Ismail wanted to say something, but kept quiet. Experience had taught him that no matter what he said next, he would not win.

"So, what do we do now?" Ismail said. "What about all the new stuff that we bought?"

"Well, the police never really asked us anything about that," Putri said. "So the stuff we paid for, we keep. The rest, well, we give back or sell it lah."

"Back to square one," Ismail said.

"I guess," Putri said.

She sighed. "You know what, though? Living with that toyol for a while… it taught me something. Do we really need to live such a materialistic life?"

"What do you mean?" Ismail asked. He did not like where this conversation was going.

"We were getting so reliant on it," Putri said. "Using it to buy so many things… but all of it clutter! How much do we really need? We were doing fine before. And I thought… maybe it's time to consider a simpler life." There was a smile on her face. "You remember my cousin? Back in my kampung?"

Ismail nodded. "Halimah? Of course."

"I'm thinking of going back and living with her. Get back to my roots. All this city life, the rat race… tak elok lah," Putri said happily. "I know a lovely little place we can move to. It's called Lembah Embun."

Ismail almost choked. "*We?* You want me to come with you?"

"Yes. I figured it might do us some good, you know? Fresh air. Going back to nature. All this wealth and materialism, what is the point of all of it?" Putri said. "Look at what happened to us. Look what happened to poor Harun."

Putri's eyes lit up as she considered the possibilities.

"We can sell our house. Sell some of the things the toyol gave us. And start a new life, as farmers! I was thinking we can start by growing kangkung, and maybe sawi too. Maybe raise some chickens."

Ismail opened his mouth again, before hurriedly closing it.

"So get better soon, sayang! Then we can start moving!" Putri said. "I'm going to buy a lot of books. I don't think there is any internet there."

Tears came to Ismail's eyes.

He hoped he could record the remaining episodes of *Crash Landing on You* before he left.

ROOFTOP, CARPATHIAN HOTEL.

"May I say," Datin Viola smiled. "Your little one is one of the prettiest toyols I have ever seen."

"Thanks so much," Dawn said.

"More tea?" The Datin took a bite of her scone.

It was another tea party on the rooftop of Hotel Carpathian. In their best summer dresses, Dawn and the Datin were enjoying a new blend of tea, this time from Morocco.

Beside them, Jungkook and the other toyols were playing a game of tag. The other toyols were fast, but he was much faster. It was not long before he tagged all of them. Their childish laughter was delightful to both women.

"Are you sure you don't want to come and work here?" the Datin said. "You seem a capable woman, and I am in need of another manager. Plus, you would already be amongst friends."

Almost all the staff of Toyols 'R' Us had been reabsorbed by Datin Viola's company. As it turned out, it took a whole village to keep the old woman happy: she needed housekeepers, bookkeepers, maids, servants, cleaners, and assistants galore.

She took high maintenance to the next level. And the Datin was more than happy to hire them all. Even Ah Chuan got a job as a concierge.

"You are too kind," Dawn smiled. "Maybe I'll consider it when I get back."

In two months, she would complete her Business degree, and then go to England to do a Masters. She had been saving for this for the past two years.

"Attagirl," the Datin smiled. "Get a good brain in that head. And go out and meet lots of people. You have the best sex of your life in university, you know. All those brainboxes. Get the passion out of their systems, before they explode!"

"I'll keep that in mind," Dawn laughed.

They took another sip from their china teacups, before Dawn spoke again.

"Actually… there is another way you can help me."

The Datin raised an eyebrow. "Really? And what might that be?"

"There's this NGO in town I've been helping out with. They're called the Women's Health Organization. They do a lot of great stuff about women's reproductive rights and so on. But they're badly underfunded," Dawn said. "They're doing a campaign called the Empowered Women's Initiative. They want to spread it all across Malaysia. I think it could do a lot of good. But they need corporate sponsors—"

"I see where this is headed," the Datin smiled. "I'm sure we can work something out. I do know a lot of hunky tycoons who owe me a favor or two." She raised her teacup. "To a beautiful partnership!"

"To a beautiful partnership!" Dawn replied. They clinked their teacups and drank.

## Kelana Jaya Fighting Pits, Selangor.

"Go! Delima!"

Fans cheered as a new contender entered the ring. Delima was a tall, gray-faced woman in a long brown dress. The long talons on her fingers glimmered in the harsh lights.

The cheers grew louder as Delima flew four feet into the air, launching herself at her competitor, the Lady Laksa. The two screamed as they slashed at each other.

At his ringside seat, Vellu Jeganathan was restless. His hands, shoved deep into his pockets, were still trembling violently.

A lot had happened in the past few days. He had been beaten up, arrested, and had his money taken from him, among other things. *But in a way*, he reflected, *all those 'misfortunes' were blessings in disguise.*

His face was still covered in bruises, and his eyes were still puffy. It would be a while before he could get back into the dating scene. The positive side of this was, he now looked so different from his original handsome self that hardly anyone could recognize him.

A shave of his head and a one mustache later, Vellu now had a new identity. Just the other day, he had passed a few Flying Daggers members outside the Pandamaran fighting pits, and none of them even batted an eyelid.

One day, he would head to the toyol pits again. He enjoyed its thrills too much; it would take an apocalypse or two to truly cut him off from there. Vellu met a bio-engineer in Klang recently, who could create toyols with skin literally ON FIRE. All those other competitors would never know what hit them!

He would be rich one day. Succeed or have his toyols die trying.

And in the meantime, there were other ways to pass the time. Such as the pontianak fighting pits. It wasn't the same as toyols, he knew. The thrills just weren't the same. But hey, it was the best thing for now!

Vellu cheered as Delima landed a particularly well-timed blow. "Bangang!" he screamed. "Get into it, you bitch! Rip her bloody eyes out! Mak kau HIJAU!!!!!!!"

Brickfields Police Headquarters.

"Razif bin Hadiman," the Legal Aid representative read his name on the documents. "Charged with possession of obscene materials."

Razif nodded. His head was shaved, and he wore an orange prison jumpsuit.

"Your hearing is tomorrow," the representative went on. "Now, I've got good news. The magistrate will likely take your age into account, and that you are a first offender. He also notes you are a budding artist with a very bright future."

Razif smiled. His 'sculpture' of Aini Hazliza had somehow made it into a gallery shortly after his arrest, and it was the talk of all the Malaysian art world. There was even talk of it winning a major art prize. Even Aini Hazliza had seen it, and posted photos of herself with it on her Instagram.

That was the thing about the Malaysian justice system. Argue that you had some sort of promising future, that you were a good student, successful athlete or even future artist (as in his case), and judges would be extremely lenient in sentencing you.

"If you plead guilty," the representative went on, "you will just need to spend several months in jail, and do community service."

Razif was silent for a while. There was only one thing on his mind.

"For that community service," he finally said, "I'd like to help out with Aini Hazliza's campaign. I would like to get to know her a little bit more."

Arun's Mamak, Bangsar.

Fara took another sip of her teh tarik. "Maybe Friday?"

"Hopefully." Khairul nodded. "If it's still playing then. You're okay with horror movies? It's not unprofessional or anything, right?"

'What? No!" Fara said. "After working hours, anything is fair game!"

She smiled: she had been doing this more often lately. Laughter was still a challenge. According to her, it made her cheeks hurt. But hey, baby steps.

Khairul and Fara were doing one of the most difficult things known to man: planning a date despite both of them having full schedules.

"You should be finished by Friday, right?" Fara asked. "Do you always take so long with your paperwork?"

"Normally, no." Khairul took a forkful of Indomie. "It's just… this report is going to be very complicated. I don't know if my boss is going to buy that it was toyols behind this."

"I guess this is one of the few aspects that my job is easier than yours," Fara said. "Evil bomohs killing people? Just another Thursday."

"I'm surprised you need to fill any paperwork at all," Khairul muttered. "Doesn't '*It was black magic*' explain everything?"

"Ah, but what kind? We have to be specific," Fara said. "Fill out spellcaster reports and so on. It's a ton of work. Some of my reports are almost like novels."

Khairul sighed. "I can't believe that even for the coolest job in the world, bloody *wizard detective*, you still need to do paperwork after. Don't you have house elves or something for that?"

Fara took another sip of her drink. "So, what are you gonna tell your boss?"

"That Ignatius was behind everything," Khairul said. "Not like the guy can argue."

Fara shuddered. They had managed to recover Ignatius's body three days after their encounter. Or at least, what was left of it. "That's not really right, is it?"

Khairul shook his head. "Ethically, no. But what else can I do? I'll say he was part of a cult or something lah. With weird practices. With that psycho manifesto of his, is that so hard to believe?"

"The media are going to *love* this story," Fara said. "If you're having any trouble with your boss, I can talk to my higher ups. They can get involved when it involves silencing occult crimes. Take the Dataran Merdeka Hellhole, for instance."

"What's that?"

"Exactly," Fara said.

According to her, Toyols 'R' Us was officially over. Her division swooped by for a raid the day after the shootout, only to find about three dozen bewildered members of staff unsure of what to do. Their boss had vanished. He wasn't answering any calls and, most shockingly, had deleted all his social media accounts! Fara had a feeling they wouldn't be hearing from him again.

"Without even a farewell note, too," Khairul shook his head. "If I were Lewis, I'd have prepared a song. I know the best one for the occasion."

Fara sighed. "And what song would that be?"

"Julio Iglesias. *Toyol the girls I've loved before….*"

There were still all the other Toyols 'R' Us branches all over Malaysia to think about. But both Fara and Khairul felt they would not last long with the disappearance of their leader.

"What are you going to do after this?" Fara asked.

Khairul shrugged. "I was thinking of taking a short vacation. Maybe Langkawi or Tioman. Cambodia, maybe, if I can afford it. After what I've seen, I need a break."

"All this too much for you?" Fara smiled.

"I don't know," Khairul said. He fidgeted with his spoon. "Before this, I was in a bit of a rut. My job was starting to feel same-ish. I needed a change." He smiled. "After this though, I may have had a bit too much change."

"Be careful what you wish for," Fara smiled. She stood up. "Well, I have to go. I'll get this one, okay?"

"Thanks," Khairul said. "See you for the movie? Whenever that is?"

"Yeah. Talk to you after my briefing. Bit of a weird case. This company in Gombak is raising the dead to work in their offices. We think it's a rogue corporate bomoh."

"Sounds serious. Sure you can't take a break?"

"Can't. We've been a bit overwhelmed. One of our officers quit recently."

She looked Khairul in the eye.

"We're looking for a competent investigator to help us out. Magical experience not even necessary. Just as long as he or she has a good eye and head for investigations. Know anyone to recommend?"

Khairul thought for a while. He took another bite of his noodles. "Do I get a phone that shoots fireballs?"

Gerwaran Apartments, Subang.

"See him yet?" Munira asked. She was lying on Jing's bed in a T-shirt and short shorts, fiddling with her smartphone.

"He should have come home by now," Jing said. She peered through the grille of her windows, only to sigh when she saw nothing.

"Maybe he got distracted," Munira suggested. "Ran into a moth or something."

"Bintang knows better," Jing said. "What if he's in trouble?"

"Eh, relax lah," Munira scoffed. "Now is not the time to be paranoid, okay?"

"I hope so." Jing sighed and sat next to Munira. She hugged her pillow tight.

"Yeah," Munira said. "Oh, by the way. Kieran just messaged me."

"Really?" Jing said, only half-interested. "What did he say?"

"It's about Tommy. He's off the team."

"What? What happened?"

"Apparently, he had a nervous breakdown," Munira said. "He didn't turn up to practice, so Kieran and a few of the guys went over. They said his room was a mess: stuff broken, furniture smashed. And Tommy was lying on his bed, in the fetal position."

"Shit," Jing said.

"Yeah. The guys went to help him and he got violent, screaming and lashing out at them. Anuar had to knock him out. He was going on and on about a 'creature'. Coach said the stress of the match was probably too much for him."

She really should have felt happy to hear this. Tommy had been a first-class jerk, and his actions almost affected her entire future. His sporting career being jeopardized should have been tit for tat.

And yet, Jing found herself feeling strangely hollow. In fact, she did not even want to think about her ex-boyfriend. Bintang had stolen his handphone yesterday, and Jing deleted all the incriminating photos. That should have been the end; Jing had even asked her toyol to return the handphone to him.

She didn't want anything to do with him anymore. There were so many other things in life worth so much more.

Just then, there was a harsh, scraping noise. Munira's eyes lit up as Jing rushed to the window.

"You're back!"

And so he was. The toyol was hanging from the drainpipe outside, his gangly limbs wrapped around it like a koala's. Jing opened the window and Bintang made a flying leap into the room, landing perfectly on his feet. He grinned to see his 'parents' and fished out a couple of grubby-looking notes from his loincloth.

"Bagus," he gurgled.

"Memang bagus!" Jing chortled, patting him on the head. His reattached hand was healing nicely—Officer Fara, that nice police officer, had introduced her to a reputable occult surgeon. He would not be able to pick up heavy objects for about three months, but after that, would be as good as new.

Having a toyol was the best. It was like having a baby, except with all the pros and none of the cons. You didn't need to buy food, clothing or entertainment for them. They spent the day sleeping in their canisters, and never woke up crying or needing to be coddled.

The best benefit of toyols, however, was that unlike babies, they brought money *in*. Bintang had spent the last three nights at the house of Munira's estranged father. The amount of jewelry and notes he had around was amazing.

"He probably owes a lot in child support, anyway," Munira said casually.

Jing wasn't sure, however, about what they were going to do with the toyol. Yes, they could just let him keep stealing ("Seriously, why not?" Munira lamented) but she knew that wasn't an option.

The pair had a few ideas. Maybe Bintang could start a lost item finding service! Or a delivery service for small items, given his speed and flexibility. Maybe he could help exterminate rats. He could track them to the tiniest crevices and feed on their blood.

They would find something for Bintang to do. But that was something to worry about later.

Munira went to the kitchen. Jing picked up her toyol, and sat down on her bed. She tickled him on the forehead, and the toyol began to cackle, sounding like a whole coop of chickens.

Munira came back from the kitchen. She was carrying a large knife.

"Are you ready, babe?"

Jing nodded and took off her shirt. Munira kissed her friend on the forehead. She raised the knife, her hands trembling slightly, and made a small cut just above her right breast. Jing winced as a small stream of blood trickled out.

Bintang's eyes lit up in delight. Within seconds, he was at his mother's breast, his tiny blackish tongue darting in and out of his mouth as it lapped up the precious blood.

"Drink well, sayang," Jing said and smiled. Munira took her hand and squeezed it tightly.

The road ahead would be difficult. But the three of them would see it through, together.

# EPILOGUE

## May 14, 4pm.
## Pasar Besar Ipoh.

The girl really wanted an ice cream. It was a hot day, and her kebaya was soaked with sweat.

She walked through the crowded market, her eyes peeled for a vendor. There was a flurry of activity all around her. People pushing wire trolleys and carrying plastic bags full of vegetables. Women selling roasted chestnuts and men selling satay. A fishmonger yelling about how fresh his fish were. People haggling with sellers over the price of clothes and shoes.

A man walked by, a lit cigarette in his mouth. The girl covered her mouth and walked away. Instinctively, her hand moved to her belly.

In three months, she would be due. The girl had no idea what she felt about that. Her boyfriend had told her not to worry too much. He would marry her, he said. And then find a good job to support them.

She didn't have too much faith in him. He had been fired from two jobs already for stealing. And showed no signs of being able to change for the better.

Births were supposed to be happy occasions. Yet the girl did not feel this was so. Her life would change forever after her baby was born, she knew. It would be the end of her blissful childhood.

What had she gotten herself into?

Suddenly, the girl noticed someone waving to her from a nearby alley.

He was a tall, dark-skinned man with a shaven head. His clothes were sharp and pressed, and he wore a single dagger-shaped earring. He smelled strongly of oranges.

"Hello there, miss," he smiled at her. His voice was smooth as honey. "I can't help notice you are pregnant. That's good, of course. But are you happy about it?"

"Why do you ask?" the girl said.

"If you're looking to get rid of it," the man said, "I can help you." He bowed. "Welcome to Toyols Sendirian Berhad! You may previously have known us as Toyols 'R' Us. We rebranded ourselves, to serve you better! My name is Lewis, and I think I can be of service!!"

"How?" the girl asked.

"So full of questions! I like you." Lewis smiled. "We're a top-secret toyol mill aimed at helping less fortunate girls like you! All you need to do is provide us with that little thing squirming in your womb. We'll pay you for it!"

"Oh," the girl said. "How much?"

Just then, a woman stepped up. She was tall, with dyed-brown hair, and wore a T-shirt and jeans. She also wore a badge: **Empowered Women's Initiative**, it read.

"Excuse me?" the woman said. "Did I hear you say you were Toyols Sendirian Berhad?"

"Indeed," Lewis said happily. "Do you want to make a toyol too?"

The woman shook her head. She had heard of organizations like his. "Come now. Don't listen to this guy. Trust me, all he wants is to make a quick buck."

She took the girl's hand gently.

"I see you're pregnant," the woman said. "And I don't know what you plan to do with your baby. Whether you keep it or otherwise, we won't judge. But whatever you decide, we will help you through it. You don't have to go through this alone."

"Thank you," the girl said gratefully. She walked away from Lewis.

"Hey!" Lewis called out. "You're missing a valuable opportunity!"

"No thanks," the girl said. "Creep."

As she and the woman turned and walked away, Lewis tried one final desperate attempt.

*"Come on! Free umbrella!"*

N
O
O
V

www.ingramcontent.com/pod-product-compliance
Lightning Source LLC
LaVergne TN
LVHW091301150826
845673LV00006B/1499

* 9 7 8 9 6 7 2 3 2 8 5 5 1 *